Who's Been Naughty or Nice?

Sonja Gunter

Published by
Satin Romance
An Imprint of Melange Books, LLC
White Bear Lake, MN 55110
www.satinromance.com

Cover Design by Ashley Byland from Redbird Designs

This book is dedicated to everyone who has been inspired by Rudolph the Red Nosed Reindeer. It is one of my favorite holiday movies to watch over and over again while I'm baking cookies.

Famous Christmas characters bring new meaning to romance with a modern day twist. Cherish this wonderful time of year in wanting to be on both Santa's nice and naughty list.

Chapter One

An aroma of peppermint filled Zane Ashcroft's senses as he inhaled. Lifting his head from the pillow, he stared at the woman he'd fallen in love with, Annie McGrath.

The love bug consumed him five years ago on his first day at Northern Polar Printing Company. He'd died and gone to heaven when the owner, Mr. North, introduced her to him. Her short, strawberry red hair, creamy complexion, and remarkable green eyes had astounded him. She'd been so calm and collected. He, on other hand, had been edgy and thought for sure she'd found him an idiot or worse, a nerd. That was a year before they began dating.

She never failed to captivate him since. Zane smiled, peering at her seductive body.

He brushed strands of hair off her face. Her eyelashes formed a dark line against her fair complexion. Up close, the prominent array of freckles spread across her nose and cheeks. He grinned. At the office no one knew she bore the attractive light brown spots, hiding them with makeup.

Zane kissed the tip of her nose and pushed down the lace strap of her blue cami, freeing one of her breasts. He cupped the mound and rubbed the nipple taut.

"Mister, what are you doing?" Her throaty-sleepy voice sent a mixture of emotions through him.

"Getting some morning delight," he murmured against her lips.

Annie's warm hand stroked his erection. Releasing her lips, he groaned. He pushed his hips to her, as jolts of pleasure pulsed through

1

him. Her magical fingers moved up and down his length.

"My, my we're anxious this morning. I was dreaming about you," she sighed.

"Oh Annie, I love you—"

Zane took command and covered her hand with his, stilling its caress. He gazed into her green eyes and opened his mouth to say more, but closed it not wanting to ruin his upcoming Christmas proposal.

She tugged her cami over her head.

Beautiful.

Exquisite.

She opened her legs and he moved in-between them. Before sliding into her warmth, he kissed her lips, nuzzled her earlobe, suckling the area just below, knowing it was her abandonment point. She moaned and her body melted.

Kissing one rosy peak then the other, he slid into her. Annie's shivers electrified him. Their hips moved in a mounting pace. Her legs wrapped around him, drawing him in closer to her softcore.

"I love you, too."

Lost in the sweetness of her declaration, a deep burning passion pushed him higher. Her shudders of ecstasy as his fingers heightened her orgasm drained all his thoughts. He brought her to her pinnacle. Her explosions radiated through him. Zane abandoned his restraint and gave into his own raw turbulent release.

Chapter Two

"Hurry up. They're saying there's a backup on Hwy 176," Annie yelled. She stood by the front door of her home tapping her foot.

"What's your hurry?"

Zane, the love of her life, leaned against the wall at the top of the stairs. Her body had a mind of its own.

His little southern twang made her knees nearly buckle, not to mention the navy suit he wore. His rich chocolate eyes were bright with mischief and his brown hair curled slightly at the wet ends. Even after their early morning lovemaking, she wanted him.

"We have our year-end meeting, remember. I still have a few reports to finalize."

"Annie, Mr. North won't be worried if you're late," Zane responded.

He descended the stairs in a manner more seductive than a model on a catwalk. She moistened her lips. He halted in front of her, pulling her into his arms. Even through the thickness of her coat she felt the bulge of his arousal. Enraptured by his very obvious desire, she reached between them to knead those contours. The scent of his fleshly showered body awakened her senses.

"You mean us, right, Mr. President." Annie almost gasped. She leaned into him, seconds away from stripping in the hallway to 'have her way with him.'

"I love you," Zane said huskily. "I'd kiss you, but I don't want to mess your lipstick."

She inhaled to pull herself together. "You're so thoughtful. Come on, let's go."

3

He released her and took his coat off the hook. Outside, their breath created white puffs, in the Chicago cold. Thankfully, he'd used the remote start and his Porsche Panamera was warm when they buckled their seatbelts.

A few minutes into their morning commute from Bull Valley to Crystal Lake, Zane broke the silence. "See, all your worrying is for nothing. The roads aren't as bad as they made them out to be. We still have time to stop at Dunkin Donuts or Starbucks for coffee if you want?"

Annie glared at Zane. His smug look raised her irritation.

He's always optimistic. She should have driven. What was she thinking?

That was the problem! She hadn't been able to think with him pulling her into his arms making her want to call in sick. She willed the image of them naked in bed all day to go away.

"I'm fine. I'll text Clarice to stop and pick up coffee. I really want to get the reports done."

"We've made our numbers plus some. Don't stress. Mr. North has already said how impressed he was with the company's financials. The Season's Greetings Charity account was a huge asset to the bottom line, which got us the Santa's Coal Company account. Remember how it made national news," Zane boasted.

"You're a great Vice President. No one can question your work ethics or abilities. Stop worrying, Annie."

"I know I shouldn't but—"

His cell phone rang cutting off her reply. He pressed the talk button on the steering wheel and maneuvered into his parking space.

"Hello, this is Zane Ashcroft."

Annie kissed his cheek, pleased with his compliment, and left him to his conversation. When she entered the green and white two-story building, she glanced over her shoulder. Zane still sat in his car.

"Good morning, Ms. McGrath," Suzy, the receptionist said and drew her attention away from Zane.

Anne couldn't help but grin. Suzy was always cheerful and smiling. Mondays most people weren't happy to be at work, but not her.

"Good morning, Suzy. Has Mr. North arrived?"

"No. Do you want me to buzz you when he does?"

"That would be great. Thanks," Annie replied and took one more glance out the window. "Mr. Ashcroft is on a call in his car. Can you tell him to stop by my office when he comes in?"

"Of course."

Annie reached up to touch a paper snowflake that hung from the ceiling. "I like what you've done to the reception area. I love these snowflakes."

"Thanks," Suzy replied. "I couldn't help myself. My granddaughters and I made several over the weekend. Nick helped hang them this morning. He's such a sweet man."

"Love 'em."

Her praise made Suzy's smile bigger. After fingering one more handmade snowflake, Annie made her way to her office. Most of the cubicles desks were still empty. She flipped on the light switch, took off her coat, and hung it on a hook on backside of the door. Then she saw Nick, the janitor.

"Oh good lord, Nick, you scared me," she exclaimed, putting her hand over her heart. "I didn't see you enter. Can I help you?"

"Didn't Mr. Ashcroft arrive with you?"

"He did."

After she spoke, she felt vaguely embarrassed, but she shouldn't since everyone knew they were a couple. Yet it wasn't anyone's business if she and Zane drove in together or not, and certainly not the company's janitor.

"I have the conference room set-up for the meeting," Nick said. "It'll be nice to see Mr. North. He doesn't come in very often anymore."

"No, he doesn't."

An awkward silence followed. She moved to her desk, but Nick continued to stand in the doorway. What did he want? Having no time to engage in a conversation, she ignored him.

"Well, you have a good morning."

"Thanks," she muttered.

He moved into the hallway and out of sight. Suzy's comment referring how nice Nick was, had her question her growing dislike of the janitor. Annie hesitated and then followed after him.

From her doorway, she couldn't see him anywhere. Her womanly

5

instincts warned her something was off with Nick. It wasn't the first she'd felt this way and this time Zane was going to listen to her concerns.

With one last glance in both directions, she returned to her desk. She removed her laptop from her briefcase and pulled up the year-end reports. As current figures updated the files, her mouth thinned in displeasure. They were well above the estimated amounts.

How had Zane known the figures before she'd entered them? What happened to transparency?

Anger seized her. A simple conversation would've quelled her irritation. What had she expected? Five years ago, miracles had happened left and right. Everything Zane said or suggested came true.

Being the VP of Finance of a company in the red, she'd always worried about being fired. Bankruptcy wasn't an uncommon word used by the employees. The old President, Mr. Bumble, had been loud, gruff, and even rude to employees and customers. He never encouraged new or technical advancements or allowed her to facilitate changes.

Then the owner, Mr. North, hired a new President, Zane, to jumpstart the company into the black. She remembered struggling to keep her cool during their introduction, not wanting to appear weak and silly in front of the man that had rendered her speechless. The serendipity of the moment threw her whole world upside down. Her instant attraction to a man she didn't know meant she'd fallen victim to love at first sight.

"Why didn't you text or call me? I could've picked up a coffee for you, too."

Annie peered away from her laptop. Clarice Donner, her staff accountant, who from the day she first hired her, was more than an employee. She was her friend, held a coffee from Starbucks.

"Oh, what time is it? I got too involved with the spreadsheets for the meeting."

"Like usual you've lost track of time. It's a few minutes before eight. I could've come early," Clarice blurted.

"No worries—" Annie stopped abruptly. Zane stood behind Clarice holding two coffees.

Clarice turned. "Good morning, Mr. Ashcroft."

"Morning, I thought she might've not called you. Here is your favorite latte." Zane chuckled. He placed both drinks on her desk. "Mr. North called. He isn't able to make the meeting in person today. We're going to do it via Go To Meetings."

She gazed up at him. A sexual surge of excitement intensified by his bold and steady meaningful stare gripped her.

Had it only been a few hours since they kissed? Since they made love.

"Annie? Is everything okay?"

Zane's words broke her delightful ambience. She blinked. "Yessss, I was... I'm wondering, if Mr. North isn't going to be coming how will—"

"If you need me to run the reports, let me know," Clarice interrupted.

"Sure, sorry. Come and see me in fifteen minutes with the bank statements." Annie spoke with fake confidence. She coughed to hide her slip. Clarice nodded and walked away.

"Don't lie, Annie. What's wrong?"

Zane's mischievous look blazed at her. He placed both hands on her desk.

"As if you need to ask. I can't think when you're this close," she uttered.

"The feeling is mutual."

She picked up the Starbucks cup with her name on it as a distraction and sipped. The thudding of her heart eased, and she remembered her earlier concern.

"Nick came to see me right after I came to my office." Annie paused, set her drink down, and rubbed her arms. "He scared me."

Zane straightened, slipping his hands into his pockets. "I've told you he's harmless." He held up a hand, stopping her. "I'll talk to him. Now finish your reports for the meeting."

He gave her one of his heart-stopping smiles, picked up his coffee, winked, and left. Annie unconsciously moistened her lips wanting him to come back and kiss her, uncaring if he ruined her lipstick.

7

Chapter Three

With purposeful strides, Zane walked to the conference room, knowing Annie's worries over the numbers were for nothing. Today was to have been a time to celebrate the company's success with the big guy. They'd still be doing so, but not in person. Timing was everything as Mr. North had taught him.

Was this another test? After all these years, Mr. North was still putting him through trial runs for the day he'd take over the entire business.

He'd first met Mr. North during his senior year of college. It wasn't until years later that Mr. North approached him about taking the President position of Northern Polar Printing Company. He'd held VP positions, but he'd never been the President of any company. After Mr. North's disclosed that the company was failing, he knew he was up for the challenge.

Most companies took Christmas as a shopping extravaganza to give them a chance to get into the black. He'd learned quickly, Northern Polar Printing was more. Their slogan, "The Magic of the Season," was spot on.

The workday had begun; several employees were at their desks, their conversations a welcome encouragement. Not only was today the principal meeting, but it was also the day they could begin to decorate their desks and areas. He wished he could somehow bottle the irresistible sounds of the festivities.

He slowed and entered the conference room. It was nicely arranged. Overcome with pride at the sight of several of the new paper products

8

and gift items displayed, he picked up an old school jack-in-the-box.

"Excuse me, Mr. Ashcroft. I've done some pre-set-up for the upcoming meeting today. Did you need me to do anything else?"

Turning, Nick stood a few feet away in his usual light gray shirt and pants.

"Everything seems to be in place. However, I haven't checked to see if the water and soda has been stocked," Zane said.

"I did. I replenished what was needed. I'll bring in buckets of ice just before the start of the meeting."

"That's great." Zane paused, debating if he should bring up Annie's trepidations. He just couldn't envision Nick acting mean or threatening. "Ms. McGrath said you were in early today."

"I was."

Nick's two-word answer wasn't what he wanted. Zane studied him with intense curiosity. Nick kept his face hidden. He couldn't read it for any emotions. Nick busied himself with a rag he'd yanked from his back pocket, running it along the table and moved around the room as if he was waiting for something or someone.

"Is there something you'd like to talk about, Mr. Pole?"

Zane hoped by using his full name, Nick would get the hint. Instead of opening up, Nick shrugged and dismissively left the room.

That was odd.

"Mr. Ashcroft, you have a call holding."

The announcement came over the conference room's intercom phone. He walked to the table, lifted the handset, and pressed the blinking light.

"Hello, Zane Ashcroft. How can I help you?"

"Good morning. Mr. Yukon, from the Gold and Silver Dreams Jewelry store. The ring you designed has arrived. Will you be able to come in and inspect it before we put the final touches on it?"

Pulling out a chair, Zane sat. Panicky, he eyed the door and spread his free hand on the table. He inhaled to stop his racing pulse. The engagement ring was ready. His plans were about to become reality.

"I can't today... Or perhaps I can at lunchtime. Yes, I'll make it happen. Say around twelve-thirty."

"I'll be here. It's unbelievably exquisite. You truly have a gift for designing."

"Thank you. Can't wait to see it myself," Zane confessed.

"I look forward to seeing you, Mr. Ashcroft," Mr. Yukon replied. "Goodbye."

"Goodbye," Zane returned and replaced the receiver.

"See what?"

Annie's surprised entrance and question startled him. He swallowed hard before turning to address her. "Oh ahhh, the room at the Hyatt for the Christmas party."

"How do you have time for that when our meeting is in a half-hour?" she exclaimed.

Thankfully, Annie didn't ask any more questions and placed red folders in front of each chair on the table. She'd taken off her suit jacket and the blouse she wore gave him a view of what he'd sampled this morning. It had been a while since they'd made love in his office or hers. Their attraction and sexual appetite had been fierce and exciting and at times they hadn't been able to control themselves. Destiny had been on their side.

When she placed a folder in front of him, she leaned in and pressed her breasts against him. He reached around and slid his hand up her calf to the hem of her skirt.

"Do all the executives get this kind of attention?" he said, huskily.

Her reply was a kiss on his neck and her hand cupping his groin. "Only the sexy ones," she whispered into his ear. "Thanks for the coffee."

She moved away, but he continued to watch her. The first couple of months he and Annie worked together, she'd been appropriately professional but reserved. When an opportunity to visit Evergreen Press, their largest customer, presented itself, he'd asked her to accompany him. She'd looked straight at him, never blinked, and said yes. The whole day, he tried to strategize a way to cancel the trip.

Would she accept his proposal? She had to.

They'd discussed the possibility of marriage on several occasions. Her objections and concerns had dwindled after time. He'd given her fair warning he would propose. She'd threatened to say no, but he felt it was only a cover on her part.

"Zane? Pay attention."

Blinking as the memories faded. "Sorry, admiring the view. Did you say something?"

"I did. I asked if you were prepared for the meeting. I don't see your reports."

"Oh crap," he roared and stood. "What time is it?"

"Goodness, what's gotten into you. It's nine-forty-five."

He hurried out the door without answering her.

Chapter Four

"Welcome to our annual year end meeting. Mr. North wasn't able to join us in person. We will, however, be using the Go To Meetings with him," Zane addressed the Directors of each department sitting around the conference table.

Annie poured herself a glass of water. Clarice was to her right. Zane sat in the middle of the table across from her. He tapped a button on an office computer. The live video streaming appeared on the conference room large screen. Annie motioned to Zane to turn down the lights.

Mr. North appeared on the screen. His white hair and beard stood out against the red polo shirt he wore. The wire-rim glasses made him appear more like Santa Claus than the owner of a modern company. Flipping open the folder, Annie straightened, ready to give her report.

"Good morning, everyone. I'm sorry I wasn't able to be there in person. However, we won't be going over the end-of-year numbers. I have exciting news. I've discovered a new company. Our merger was signed earlier this morning. The ink hasn't even dried yet. The new company will be a huge asset to next year's bottom line. Now I'd like to introduce, Mr. Moonracer."

Suddenly a big burly man with brown hair and a short beard appeared. "Hello, I, too wish I could've been there in person, but due to the time of the season I have a very busy schedule. Mr. Ashcroft, I hope to meet with you soon. Ms. McGrath, it'll be a pleasure to open up my company books to you. To everyone else in the room, hello."

"Mr. Moonracer, I look forward to that day," Zane said.

Annie glanced at him. He met her stare and shrugged his shoulders.

12

Frustrated beyond belief, she pursed her lips. Mr. North reappeared on the screen.

"Now with that out of the way, I want to congratulate everyone on a successful year. I will be at the company's Christmas party. Mr. Moonracer and I have a lot more to finalize. I'll be cutting the meeting short. Have a great day." Mr. North then rumbled, "Ho, ho, ho."

The screen went dark. Annie stared at the blank screen not sure what to make of the year-end meeting. She saw she wasn't alone.

Clarice nudged her. "That's it?"

Zane stood, turned up the lights, and walked over to the display of items. "As you saw, Mr. North is busy, but I too, want to thank everyone for a job well done. You've all worked very hard to make this year more profitable and the company's risen to new levels." He lifted the company's number one seller item. "Without the success of our remake of the vintage Dollee doll, we'd be back to square one in the creation of new ideals. Dollee has been more profitable than even I could have imagined. Each of the employees will receive one as a thank you. All will have a numbered tag and a special note from Mr. North in remembrance of the milestone."

A round of applause interrupted his remarks. Annie could only half-smile.

Why hadn't he shared this with her? Why had he kept her in the dark?

Resentful, she tapped her finger on the file in front of her.

"Okay." Zane cleared his throat. "Okay now." The noise level softened, and he continued. "These few weeks before Christmas should be exciting. Let's make this year more memorable. Thank you again for all your hard work."

Annie sat stone-faced, fuming. She'd stressed over the numbers for weeks and no one even cared or thought she should know they were considering an acquisition. Slapping the red folder on the table, she rose and glared at Zane. She walked out of the room, nearly running Nick down. His fingers bit into her arms. If it wasn't for the protection of her suit jacket she was sure to have had bruises.

"Ms. McGrath you shouldn't be in such a hurry."

"Oh for the love of—"

13

"Nick, can I help you?"

Annie jerked out of Nick's grip. Zane stilled her by placing his hand on her lower back.

"She ran into me," Nick barked. Then as if he realized he'd been rude, he changed his tone. "It was time for me to see if more ice was needed."

Not to be intimated, Annie moved farther from the two men's reach. "I have work to do."

Chapter Five

"Annie," Zane shouted.

Her stiff back told him now wasn't the right time to go after her. Her temper would have to cool first. He'd tried to tell her not to worry about the meeting, when he'd brought her coffee, but she hadn't listened. Mr. North had asked him not to say anything, and business ethics always took precedence over their private relationship.

Zane turned his attention to Nick. "Sorry, but our meeting is over."

"Oh, that was short. Mr. North was a no show?"

Nick's question was laced with a tone of contempt, making Zane realize Annie might be right.

"He couldn't be here in person. He had other business to attend to," Zane explained.

"I was hoping to talk to him. You know, to wish him a happy holiday."

"You, along with everyone else," Zane said with false cheerfulness. "You'll get a chance at the Christmas party."

A few of the Directors came out into the hall, halting Nick's response.

"Mr. Ashcroft, this is so exciting. I've wanted a Dollee doll since the art department showed us," Clarice expressed.

"Yes, me too."

"My wife is going to be so surprised."

Zane redirected his eyes to her and the others. "You're welcome. Nick can you—"

"What does Mr. Moonracer's company make?"

"We couldn't find anything on the internet."

Zane scanned the area for Nick, but he'd vanished. Once again business came first. Smiling, he led the group into the conference room.

For a good half-hour he chatted with the Directors. He shared that Mr. Moonracer's company was very private. It dealt in all kinds of forgotten items, by purchasing the expired or expiring patens. The company's art and design departments would then modify, add newness to the old items, and market them. The room filled with oohs and aahs. He promised to fill them in with more details after the first of the year.

They nodded and grinned as the room cleared. Zane took a deep breath, about to sit when he noticed the time. Twelve-ten.

Crap! He was late to see the ring.

Hurriedly, Zane stopped to grab his coat and paused to tell Suzy he was going to lunch. The drive to downtown Crystal Lake didn't take long. Parking was worse. The one-way street only offered minimal spaces. After two turns around the block, a spot finally opened. Mr. Yukon was waiting as he entered the store at twelve-forty.

"Sorry, I'm late," Zane said.

"No worries, Mr. Ashcroft. I'll pull the ring from the vault."

Zane paced around the jewelry store. Clarice had helped him by bringing Annie here on the premise of exploring ideas for a gift for her mother's sixty-fifth birthday. She'd also been inspirational in arranging special things for their hotel room.

"Here you go," Mr. Yukon announced.

Halting his pacing, Zane's nerves took over and his feet were glued to the floor.

"I think the three carat diamond will add to the beauty of the emeralds and rubies. If you go any bigger, you'll have to do so with the other jewels."

Inhaling, Zane stepped to the counter. The ring lay against a black velvet board. He picked up the gold band. The four-baguette emeralds, two on each side, with a spray of rubies, sparkled.

His plan to propose to her at the company's Christmas party inspired him to design a ring that would symbolize a poinsettia, which was Annie's favorite plant. He wanted it to be truly unique, but not over the top.

"It's exactly as I imagined."

Mr. Yukon smiled. "I'm glad. I have the diamond here, too." He opened a piece of white paper to reveal a pear shaped diamond. "It's flaws are almost non-existence. It took me months to find one I thought worthy of presenting to you."

"Again, thank you. I'd like to pick it up on December twelfth."

"It'll be ready," Mr. Yukon promised. "Just call and I'll make sure I'm here myself."

Zane turned the ring around. He set it down on the black velvet board and took the diamond from Mr. Yukon. Anticipation took hold. Handing back the diamond, Zane grinned.

Annie was sure to say yes.

Chapter Six

In disgust, Annie grabbed her coat, but then remembered she didn't have her car. She replaced her coat and sat at her desk with her hands clenched in her lap.

How could he have excluded her from such important news? Resentment and hurt clouded her thoughts. His earlier praise curdled in her stomach. She'd worked hard over the years to prove herself valuable in the corporate world.

Logging on to her laptop, she surfed the internet for Mr. Moonracer. Nothing.

It was as if the man and his company were non-existence. Unwilling to concede, she searched harder. She googled outdated toys, not vintage. Then an image of Mr. Moonracer popped up. Her eyebrows rose. The picture was from the nineteen-twenties and the man hadn't changed.

"Isn't it wonderful we all get a Dollee doll?"

Annie looked up at Clarice, dismissing the man in the picture, as being a relative. "I have work to do. No time to chat."

"Come on, you do have admit it was very thrilling how Mr. Ashcroft kept it a secret, even from you. That's what makes the surprise super special."

Tightening her lips, Annie shook her head. "It's not how I saw it. I'm the vice president. I should have been included."

Clarice moved to the chair in front of her desk and sat. "A man who can keep a secret wins points in my book, any day. Do you need me to help you do anything before I start decorating?"

"Joy. Joy. Joy. Not today."

18

"Okay, but remember Santa has lots of helpers to let him know who's been naughty or nice," Clarice said with authority.

"Aren't you a little old to still believe?"

Laughing, Clarice put her hands on her hips. "Look who's talking. The woman who gets to sleep with Santa every year after our Christmas party."

Annie couldn't help herself and smiled. Mister Santa, AKA/Zane Ashcroft, President of Northern Polar Printing Company was her lover/boyfriend/wanna be fiancée, if he had his way. She wasn't even sure what people over forty called their significant other now days. Clarice had brought up a good point, she hadn't thought about it like that before.

"It still doesn't give him the right to not trust me."

"Trust? That should never come into play. He trusts you, it's—"

"You don't have to defend him," Annie protested. "Go put up your decorations. Enjoy this time."

Clarice stood. She opened her mouth to say more, but didn't and left. Annie pondered her co-worker's actions. Lifting her coffee, she sipped but grimaced. The cold liquid wasn't worth swallowing. Rising, she went to the break room.

"Ms. McGrath, why didn't you tell us about the gift from the company?"

Annie paused, turned to the employee, and took a deep breath. "It wouldn't have been a surprise. I'm glad you liked it."

"Thank you again, I will."

She hadn't taken more than two steps and was confronted by a different employee.

"I just heard, Ms. McGrath. Thank you."

"Charlie, you're welcome. Without the art department she would never have become a reality. Keep up the great work."

The older man eyes become bright. He nodded and continued on his way. Annie hurried to the break room not making eye contact with anyone and got a fresh cup of coffee. On the way back to her office, she saw Zane rush out of his. Instead of going to hers, he went in the opposite direction to the reception area and left the building.

Now what's going on? More secrets?

19

Five years ago, at the age of thirty-seven the 'M' word would've had her high tailing away from Zane. She hadn't really been looking for a man, boyfriend, or a relationship. Many years prior to that, she'd come to a decision that sharing her life with one single man wasn't worth the trouble. Casual dating fit into her lifestyle and she couldn't imagine ever wanting to marry. She'd been alone and happy in her hunky-dory Annie world. Now that Zane was a major part of her life, she wondered if she'd misjudged the man with whom she'd been talking about making a lifelong commitment.

Back in her office, she took matters into her own hands and called him. The call went directly to voicemail. She hung up. Fuming, Annie paced her office.

"You're thinking awfully hard in here."

Pausing, Annie glared at Clarice.

"Oh my, what's wrong?" Without an invite, Clarice came in and sat down.

Disconcerted Annie crossed her arms and looked away. "I have a headache and I can't go home, because I rode in with Zane."

"I have ibuprofen."

Full-fledged into her lie, Annie bluffed away. "I took some. I'll be fine. Don't worry."

"Did you want to go to lunch? Some food should help. I could pick up something."

Clarice's cheerfulness gnawed at her uncertainties. Annie sat in her chair. "Maybe a Cobb Salad with chicken. Thank you."

"No problem," she paused, peeked over her shoulder, and then continued. "What do you think of the security guard Rudy?"

Blinking to redirect her thoughts, Annie grinned. "He's very polite."

Clarice stood abruptly. "I'll go get our lunch."

"Hold on a minute. Why are you asking?"

"Never mind. Gotta go."

"Oh we'll talk about it when you get back," Annie said to Clarice's retreating figure.

Glancing out the window, which gave her a view of the parking lot, she saw Zane still hadn't returned. More suspicion took hold. Twenty minutes later, Clarice arrived with their lunch. They unwrapped their salads, neither saying anything. Annie kept hoping Clarice would bring up something about her earlier comment, regarding the security guard.

"If you thought I'd forgotten about your Rudy question, I didn't," Annie declared.

With a mouth full of salad, Clarice went and shut the door. "It's nothing. The other day when I left for the day he smiled at me. You know men usually do because of these—girls." She chuckled and waved her hand in front of her double-D breasts. They were thrust tight against the V-neck blouse she wore.

"Of course any red-blooded male would drool over them, natural or bought. If you want, I can request a background check on him from the N & N Security Company."

"You'd do that for me?"

"Yes," Annie assured her, dabbing her mouth with a napkin.

"No, you better not."

"Clarice, I'm not the person to give dating advice."

"Why not? I know you're the boss, but we're friends. I don't want to jeopardize my job or our friendship. I've never dated anyone I worked with before, it's..."

"I get it. I didn't either until I met Zane. It does have its ups and downs."

They grew quiet both deep in thought. Annie finished her salad and peered out the window. His parking place remained empty. He hadn't even come to apologies before he'd left or called her back. She hadn't left a message, but her number would've shown on the caller ID. Then she realized she'd used the office phone instead of her cell. Tempted to call him again, she decided to wait.

A tap on her door interrupted their lunch. Suzy came in carrying a box. "Sorry, I was told to drop off these decorations to your office."

Clarice took the box. "Great. Thanks, I'll start in on them. We're done with lunch."

"Ms. McGrath, Mr. Ashcroft said to tell you he had an important meeting and will be gone most of the afternoon," Suzy said.

"Thank you."

Suzy nodded and left. Clarice cleaned up their leftover lunch and, without saying any further words, took the box and went to her desk.

Annie tapped the shift button, bringing her laptop to life. The clock showed ten after one.

Where could he be? This wasn't like him.

The more time passed the madder she got. Three o'clock became four, and then five came and went. Preparing to call a taxi, she began to plan what she was going to say to the man who held her heart, but didn't trust her.

Chapter Seven

Lying to Annie wasn't an option. Zane went to the Hyatt Regency O'Hare Hotel to speak with the event planner. Their quick talk took over an hour and half. Then it was five o'clock. The traffic back to the office on the other side of Crystal Lake was stop and go. He thought about calling Annie a million times, but didn't think it would help him at this point.

He pulled into the company's now empty parking lot. Annie's office was the only one with the light on and the blinds shut. Using his keys, he went through the front entrance. Since he'd left this morning, the place had been transformed into a holiday extravaganza. Christmas trees and snowman of all sizes along with elves made the rooms a festive treat. He made his way slowly to Annie's office, unprepared to talk to her.

She stood next to a filing cabinet with no shoes on, her suit coat off, and her sleeves rolled up.

"Are you ready to go home?"

Annie's back stiffened before she spoke. "In a minute. I'll have to cancel my taxi."

She didn't turn, just kept pushing files back and forth.

"Annie, I'm sorry—"

"I don't want to hear it. I'll be ready in five minutes."

Her dismissal evident, Zane tapped his hand on the doorframe, deciding if he should press the conversation. "Okay, we can talk in the car."

No acknowledgment came from her. He walked to his office and heard the file drawer slam shut. There'd only been one other time he'd

23

experienced her temper and knew it was a hard thing to soften at this point.

Exactly five minutes later, he went to her office. She was waiting in the hallway. When she saw him, she flipped off the light switch and walked to the front.

"Annie," he called out.

She didn't slow, just pushed the metal bar on the door, and went out into the cold. He caught the door before it hit him. Zane pressed the remote start and unlocked buttons. She was already buckled in when he got to the car.

After adjusting the temperature and the radio, he turned to her. "I'm sorry I made you wait."

"Just drive me home. I don't want to talk."

Even in the darkness, he knew her face had hardened. He put the car in reverse and then drive. Their twenty-minute ride was completed in silence until he parked in her driveway.

"There's no need for you to come inside. We need a break from each other—time to think about our relationship."

He heard her choke over the last words. She still didn't look at him. She unbuckled her seatbelt and left the car. He watched her walk to the front door where she paused. He held his breath as he waited for her to turn, but she didn't. She opened the door and went inside, closing it behind her.

Zane hit the steering wheel. Granting her request was the hardest thing he'd done in a very long time. Light snow began to fall as he drove across town to his home. Several ideas came to him on how to resolve their argument.

Flowers? No, too predictable. Box of Norman Loves Chocolate? No, too cheesy.

More things came to mind, but as the song "The Twelve Days of Christmas" played on the radio, it triggered a plan. He'd use cards as the twelve days before his proposal. The numbers would work if he started tomorrow. He'd have to swing by Walgreens before work.

His two-story brick house loomed in front of him. It was not his home any longer. He'd been spending so much time at Annie's and making her home theirs. Opening the door, cold greeted him. He cranked up the thermostat and went into the kitchen, starting the Krups' coffee machine. It spitted and hissed. He reached for a coffee cup as the doorbell rang.

"Coming!"

Spilling the coffee he'd just poured, he hurried to the front door, unsure who it could be.

"Mr. North?" Zane eyeballed a red limo parked in the street. It stood out like a beckon against the grayness.

"Zane, I hope I'm not disrupting anything."

"No, no. Come on in." He held open the door. "Sorry about the chillness, I turned up the heat."

"A little cold isn't going to hurt me."

"I don't have much in the house to offer you. I haven't been grocery shopping in days. I just made coffee, would you like a cup?"

"That works for me."

Zane led him into the kitchen. It wasn't the first time Mr. North had shown up at his doorstep, but tonight of all times was odd. He poured another cup of coffee and wiped up the earlier spillage from the counter top.

"I know it's late, but I flew here right after concluding business with Mr. Moonracer. I felt not everyone was happy at my announcement."

"You're right. Annie... Ms. Ashcroft, didn't like being kept out of the loop," Zane confessed and sat in one the high back chairs.

"Oh, I see."

Leaning on one elbow, Zane rested his head on his hand. "As a matter of fact, she's fuming."

Mr. North laughed and went to the refrigerator. He took out a carton of cream and poured some into his coffee.

Zane wondered when he'd gotten that. He hoped it was still good.

"She'll understand soon. She's been on my Nice List for a very long time. I've kept an eye on her."

Zane straighten his shoulders. "A Nice List? I'm not a kid. This whole day has been peculiar from the start. Now it's ending even weirder. I've appreciated everything you've done for me, but now isn't the time for your—"

"Zane, the time has come for you to know the truth."

Mr. North pushed his glasses back to the bridge of his nose and laughed as he pulled his earlobe.

A delightful smell of cookies flooded the kitchen. Zane inhaled and stared wide eyed at him.

Chapter Eight

Annie leaned against the door and let the tears fall. She'd held them in all day. Several times during the ride home, being so close to him, she'd forced them back. How could she love a man who didn't trust her? Locking the door, she hung up her coat and walked up the stairs to the bedroom.

More tears fell as she stared at the unmade bed. Zane's robe lay on the floor next to the bed. She picked it up and inhaled. His scent remained strong on the fabric. Carrying it into his closest, she laid it across the dressing stool, and shut the door.

Shedding her suit and blouse, she turned on the faucet to fill the tub and added oil. In her panties and bra, she sat on the tub edge.

She should call him. Tell him to come over.

No. They needed time. Turning off the faucet, she disrobed and sank into the hot water, allowing it to encase her body. She sighed and rested her head against the tub back. The soothing water eased away some of her tension. Forty-five minutes later, wrapped in a towel she curled up in the lounge chair and fell asleep.

A beeping sound woke Annie. Her foggy brain didn't register it as the alarm until she stumbled from the chair. Hitting the stop button on the clock, she exhaled. The silence was golden. She wiped sleep from her eyes and surveyed her surroundings.

She'd slept in the lounge chair the entire night. Not the bed that just yesterday she'd shared with Zane. The bed in which they'd made love, not once, but three times.

Readjusting the bath towel, she searched for her phone. Annie headed down the stairs, and the beeping started again. Ignoring the alarm clock, she found the cell phone in her purse by the front door. Opening it, no missed calls, or test messages showed on the screen. Tossing it back into her purse pocket, she went back to her bedroom and put an end to the relentless beeping. With a sad heart, she got ready to go to work alone.

She checked her phone again as she put on her coat. Still nothing. Grabbing her keys from the hall table she went to the garage. Her BMW 750 came to life with a press of a button.

Traffic was heavy and she couldn't stop for coffee. Zane's Porsche was in his spot and only a few other cars were in the parking lot. Going straight to her office, she realized her light was on. Cautiously, Annie moved toward the doorway as thoughts of Nick being in her office made her nervous. Her room was empty. But a Starbucks venti coffee was on her desk with a card leaning against it. Hanging up her coat, she peeked into the hallway. Light shown into the hallway from Zane's office. She could tell by the way that a shadow would appear, he was inside.

Should she go see him?

Her mind worked through several scenarios. Finding none she liked, Annie walked to her desk and picked up the coffee. The cup was warm to the touch. Taking a sip, she found the liquid wasn't warm, but hot. Fingering the card, she lifted it, sniffing. An easy smile cased her lips. The envelope had Zane's signature cologne, Drakkar, lingering on it. Sliding her finger under the lip, she tore it open.

A woman in a spa towel wrap was on the front of the card. Opening it, a gift card fell to her desk. She read the handwritten message.

Enjoy a day to ease away the stress. Maybe next time I'll be able to give you a massage, Love Zane.

Her determination to stay mad faded, but she remained unwilling to tell him. Letting him suffer a while longer would be punishment enough.

Annie shoved the two cards into her desk drawer.

The morning turned into the afternoon and she still hadn't made time to go see Zane. She'd heard his voice several times as the employees thanked him about the Dollee doll.

At lunchtime, she planned to confront him, but Clarice brought in salads. One more chance gone. They ate while discussing the company's Christmas party. With most of the plans complete, it was just the fine details, which for some unknown reason were her responsibility. She was tempted to tell Zane to give it to some other department next year.

"Can we have male strippers dressed as elves serving us?"

Clarice's question brought Annie's roaming thoughts to halt. "No, but the wait staff could be dressed as elves. It will complete the winter wonderland theme."

"I thought that suggestion might get your attention. You weren't listening to a word I said for a few minutes. Everything okay?"

Annie closed her eyes and pushed her hair behind her ears. "It's been a long day. I don't want to think about the party anymore. We can take it up tomorrow. I'm going home."

"Sure, you do look tired." Clarice chuckled as she stood and went to her desk.

Her friend's assessments were right, but not for the reason she was implying. It was really from lack of sleep and a lonely night. Turning off her laptop, Annie shut it. Deciding to leave her computer, she picked up her briefcase and folded her coat over her arm. In the hallway, she spotted Zane heading out to the warehouse. Her earlier forgiveness now gone, aggravation that he hadn't come to talk to her held sway.

She missed him. She left the building and headed home, confused.

Chapter Nine

Out of the corner of his eye, Zane saw Annie leaving as he went to the warehouse. Several times during the day he'd been about to talk to her, but then thought better of it. She'd requested her space and he was going to honor it. From the warehouse windows he watched her getting to her car.

"Mr. Ashcroft, we've run into a problem."

Zane turned. Mr. Elfner, the warehouse-shipping manager stood next to him.

"What kind of problem?"

"Several of the label machines have been vandalized."

"Vandalized? That's a harsh statement."

Mr. Elfner nodded. "Come this way."

As they walked, Mr. Elfner continued to talk while they hurried to the docking area.

"We started the day like any other. The orders printed. They were picked, packed, and labeled, but when it came to verifying the manifest we couldn't get it to print. Upon investigation, we found the computers were unplugged. Some of the wiring had been tampered with and can't be fixed until the IT department gets here. The UPS trucks are waiting to be loaded with today's packages. We're so far behind—"

"Slow down," Zane said. "We'll do it by hand, if we must. Page all the employees to the warehouse."

In five minutes almost one hundred office and warehouse employees had gathered ready for instructions. Zane took a bullhorn from Rudy.

"Thank you all for coming. As you know this is our busy time of the year. The shipping department needs our help. Our manifest isn't working. I need everyone to help record the orders via the bar codes. They're ready to be loaded onto the UPS trucks. I can't stress the importance of these orders going out today."

Mr. Elfner handed out pens, papers, and a few IPad's instructing the employees to go to the carts. By seven thirty, all orders were loaded, hand checked, and pictures taken of each bar code. A round of cheers echoed through the warehouse by the last thirty plus employees who'd stayed until the end.

"Thank you everyone. I've been assured the manifest will print for tomorrow's orders," Zane yelled.

He was proud of the teamwork. As the employees began to leave his phone beeped. Excited, thinking it was from Annie, it vanished when he saw a text from Mr. North.

```
Great job. We'll talk more tomorrow.
```

How had he known about the problem? Zane typed.

```
Thank you. I do have a few questions
about what we discussed last night.
```

A thumb up emoji was Mr. North's reply.

Zane checked to see if he had missed a message from Annie, but he hadn't. He bit the bullet and texted her.

```
Busy day. Sorry I missed you today. See
u in the morning.
```

Tapping send, he waited for her reply. A minute passed and none came. Disheartened, he pocketed his phone.

Mr. Elfner thanked him and then said goodbye. Zane wandered the warehouse, checking the shelves of inventory. Mr. North's explanation that Northern Polar Printing was only a small part of his vast enterprise wasn't news to him. A man as affluent as Mr. Chris North was had to have other business ventures. The tabloids were always speculating on what Mr. North's net worth was and bringing up at this time of year his resemblance to the seasons icon Santa.

The farther Zane walked, the more he failed to make sense of their late night conversation. Mr. North had rambled on and on about the history of Christmas and how extraordinary things happen. He hinted that a big change was about to happen.

Zane couldn't remember Mr. North leaving or how he'd gotten into bed. He put it out of his mind assuming it had been all the late night caffeine and exhaustion. As he made his way to his office, he realized most of the employees who'd stayed late had left. After finalizing a few reports and emails, he called it a day at nine o'clock.

He drove by Annie's house. Seeing most her lights were lit, Zane parked down the street, and sent another text.

```
Good night. Luv u.
```

Again, he waited, but this time after a half hour elapsed Zane realized no response was coming and headed home. Tonight his house was the same as yesterday, quiet. Disliking the darkness, he turned on several lights and, for background noise, clicked on the surround sound music. Having not really eaten a meal all day, he went in search of something to fill his complaining stomach.

The empty refrigerator wasn't helpful. He hadn't had time to go grocery shopping again. However, in the freezer he found a box of Eggos. They were a little freezer burnt, but they were better than nothing.

After toasting two, he spread a thick layer of peanut butter on them and carried them into the den. Country Christmas music played and he soon fell asleep only to be awakened by a chirping sound. Quickly, he ran to get his phone from his coat pocket. Bringing his phone to life, he saw Annie had sent a message, time stamped a minute past midnight.

```
Nite.
```

A simple word, but it was all he needed. Now fully awake, he opened his briefcase and took out the stack of eleven cards he'd purchased yesterday. His twelve cards before his proposal plan had to work. The Day Two Card featured two nutcracker soldiers and when it opened, *The Nutcracker's,* theme song played. Printed inside was, *Let's go a little nuts.*

Zane thought for a moment and then wrote his message.

I'll share mine,
Love Zane.

Smiling, he sealed the card.

Chapter Ten

Driving by the Starbucks the next morning, Annie didn't consider stopping. If Zane really cared for her, there would be one sitting on her desk. For hours last night she'd weighed comment after comment to text him. Each one had sounded desperate and she ended up replying with a simple good night. No emoji's, x's, or o's. After hitting send she'd waited for his response, but had fallen asleep holding the phone.

Like every day, Suzy was her normal, cheerful self. As Annie made her way to her office, the chatter level was high for the morning. When she flipped on the light, there on her desk was the coveted coffee, accompanied by another card. She smiled, despite being mad at Zane. Today, after she hung up her coat she sat, enjoyed several sips of the still warm latte, and opened the card.

Nutcracker soldiers adorned the front reminding her of the time she and Zane had gone to the Chicago Theater to see the play. Opening the card, it played the theme song. His private message about sharing nuts had her wishing she hadn't banned him from her bed.

With her coffee and card in hand, she walked to Zane's office only to find he wasn't there. Annie searched the hallway. Disappointed, she went to his desk and wrote, thanks, on a yellow sticky. She stuck it to his coffee cup. Returning to her office, she found Clarice waiting.

"Can we talk about the Christmas party?"

Annie nodded and sat.

"Good, cause yesterday you weren't paying attention," Clarice said.

Ignoring the remark, Annie opened the Christmas expense file. "We're within the planned budget. There's room for additional expenditures. Is there something you want to change or add?"

"There is. I was thinking—"

"Good morning, ladies."

34

In unison Annie and Clarice glanced toward the doorway.

"Morning, Mr. Ashcroft," Clarice said.

"Can you give Ms. McGrath and me a few minutes?"

Annie eyed Zane suspiciously.

"Of course," Clarice replied, stood, and sidestepped past Zane with her mouth open, closing the door behind her.

Pressing her lips, Annie forgot her apprehension as to why he wanted to see her alone. Zane looked very handsome today in his gray suit. It was one of her favorites on him.

She struggled for control.

She moistened her lips. He stepped over to her desk in a scandalous strut. She eyed his hips. His pleated slacks hid his package. She didn't need the outline to envision what she couldn't see.

"I see you got my card this morning."

His smooth sweet voice sent a delicious shudder through her. Annie blinked, pushing the sexual fantasy to the depths of her mind. Unwilling to let him know she was softening, she opened her laptop.

"Thank you again. It was a nice surprise."

"I've missed you. I'm trying to honor your request, but it's hard. If you want, I can get tickets to the Nutcracker."

Avoiding his soft caressing stare, she tapped on the keyboard. "No, that's okay, I'm not sure I'll have time for nut—"

"We could go as kind of a date?"

Her words had sounded forced. She missed him terribly. Having him stand in front of her, so close she could touch him, smell his cologne, she fought for her space and a meaningful apology.

He reached across her desk and put his hand over hers. "When you're ready, I'll be here for you."

His fingers lingered for a moment, and then he walked out of her office. She released the breath she'd been holding.

Clarice came in about a split-second later. "Oh my, you're one lucky lady."

"Stop it. He is the President and I'm the VP."

"That doesn't change the facts." Clarice giggled.

"Now isn't the time to discuss my personal affairs. Did you still want to talk about the party?"

For over an hour they made tiny changes to the big night to fine tuning the food selections and the company gifts to each employee.

"This is going to be the best ever party," Clarice declared.

Annie made a few note and closed the file. "Guess what?"

"What?"

"We have twelve months to plan next years."

"I can hardly wait. I love all this. Maybe someday I'll start my own party planning company. What do you think?"

With furled eyebrows Annie stared at Clarice. "I could see that. I'd start out small. Market yourself. Get a website. If you get it going, I can see if we could hire you next year."

Clarice jumped from the chair, excitement foremost. "Really? Oh my gosh, that would be totally awesome."

"Settle down. Everyone's looking over here." Annie laughed. "I think you have it in yourself to succeed. I knew you'd move on to something else soon."

"This is the best Christmas gift ever. Oh my, I have to get a business plan."

Clarice literally bounced out of the office. Her excitement was off the charts. Annie too left her office and walked by Zane's, but he wasn't there. Deciding to check on an inventory problem herself, she went to the warehouse.

It was lunchtime and the forklifts along with the conveyor belts were shut down. Her high heels clicked and echoed as she walked to Aisle twenty-six.

As she neared it, a noise to the right caught her attention. She stopped. "Hello?"

Surveying the area and listening, she saw and heard nothing. She approached the aisle and walked down the row. Again, she heard more noise and hesitated. This time an odd odor greeted her.

Cookies?

Had an employee taken their lunch break back here? Cautiously, she stepped to the end of the isle.

"Hello? Who's there?"

No reply came but from the corner of her eye, she saw a man.

"Mr. North?"

Turning to get a better look, she found the space was empty. Her imagination was playing tricks on her.

"Ms. McGrath, what are you doing this far in the warehouse?"

Twisting, she faced Nick, who was coming toward her. "Oh goodness, I thought I just saw Mr. North. Were you the one making noise?"

"Mr. North? Here? When did he arrive?"

"He hasn't as far as I know." Annie exhaled hard. "Never mind."

"Annie? I've been looking for you."

Zane voice brought relief. Nick stopped his advance and left as Zane passed him. She hadn't realized she'd been holding her breath and gasped when she released it.

"I'm checking on an inventory problem. I was caught up and didn't want to bother anyone."

"I'll page Mr. Elfner. Come on. Have you eaten?"

The roar of engines interrupted the quietness. "No, I will in a bit. Do you smell that?"

"Smell what?"

Pursing her lips, she put her hands on her hips. "Why is everyone answering my questions with a question? Excuse me."

Lowering her hands, she walked by him. He followed her only to the door.

The afternoon came and went. Annie found herself in unfamiliar territory. After her encounter with Zane and Nick, she hadn't seen either of them. Zane's standoffish attitude wasn't what she wanted when she'd asked for a little space. Looking out the window, their cars were the only ones in the parking lot.

Did that mean they were the only ones left in the building? She should go to him. She was being childish.

Her phone rang. The caller ID showed it was Zane.

"Hello, Annie McGrath."

"Can you come to my office before you leave?"

"Yes. I'll be there in a few minutes," Annie replied.

"Okay."

They hung up. Leaning back in her chair, she wondered what was so important this late in the day. Turning everything off, she took her coat, and briefcase, and headed to his office. She knocked on his open door. He stood, motioning for her to enter. He'd taken off his suit coat and had loosened his red paisley tie. She walked to him hesitantly, wanting to rip off his confining tie and shirt.

Had it only been forty-eight hours since we'd made love?

Her irrational sexual drive made her wonder if all women in their forties went through wanting a man every hour of the day. It was ludicrous.

He took her coat and briefcase from her and set them on the chair in front of his desk. "I have to leave tonight. Mr. North wants me in International Falls. I'll be gone a couple of days—three to be exact."

She clasped her hands behind her, afraid she'd fling herself at him.

Gone for days! They haven't made-up yet.

"Is there anything I can do, or that you want me to do while you're gone?"

Zane invaded her personal space, putting his hand on her waist, pulling her against him. His mouth firm, silencing her rejection. The kiss was a drug, burning a fire through her veins. Of their own accord, her hands wound themselves around him. Drinking in his smothering and demanding lips. Her anger faded, along with her selfishness. In its place, an uncontrollable hunger.

Unable to resist, she slid her hand over his butt cheeks and gave one side a pinch. Having the desired effect, his bulging erection pressed into her. Their clothes a hindrance, his hand found its way under her skirt and his fingers caressed the area protected by her satin underwear. Spreading her legs, one then two fingers brushed aside the barrier, sliding into her wetness. A moan escaped her, breaking the sexual tension.

In a surprising action, he lifted her and carried her to the leather couch. The initial intimacy was lost as he sat her down. Swinging her legs to the front, Annie adjusted her skirt and blouse.

"I'm not sure this is the right thing to do, Zane."

His response was to shut and lock his door. She watched as he closed the blinds, and sauntered over to her while shedding his shirt and tie. Shutting out the image of his broad chest, she stood, and took a step toward the door, but found herself back in his embrace, pressed against the wall.

Their lips met. She parted hers, abandoning all her commonsense, and giving into the ecstasy. Pushing her skirt up, Zane knelt in front of her, pulling her panties down to her ankles. Bracing against the wall, her hands dug into his hair as his lips and tongue kissed her mound. Her senses short-circuited, making her knees tremble. He shoved two fingers into her core, suckling her clitoris. Panting, she squirmed, but he held her steady as her world spun and the first tremors seized her.

"Ohhh Zane, I'm ready now."

The first explosive orgasm came. He didn't stop his magic and a second one followed. In between her hard breathing, she was coming back to reality only to feel his manhood penetrate deep inside her.

Annie screamed when her third heart-stopping explosive release matched his. Their labored breathing was the only sound in the room.

"I love you." Zane sighed.

Slowly she opened her eyes. He was staring at her.

"This doesn't mean I'm forgiving you."

"If this wasn't makeup sex, I can't wait for the real thing." He grinned and moved away allowing her to readjust her clothes as he did the same.

Annie laughed. He had a way of knowing the right thing to say. She should feel embarrassed or even cheapened by what had happened, but didn't. Their passionate lovemaking had been special.

He picked up his shirt and tie and dressed. "This wasn't the reason I asked you to come to my office," he said as he buttoned his shirt.

"Why did you?"

"To tell you I have to leave and that I wanted to give you something." He tucked in his shirt, opened a desk drawer, and pulled out some envelopes. "These are cards. I want you to open one each day I'm gone. They're labeled. Tomorrow will be the Day Three Card."

"Zane this is crazy."

"I know, but you reminded me you still haven't forgiven me. I'm going to give you a card a day with the last one being the most important."

Annie didn't know what to say. Was he hinting at a proposal again?

"Here take them."

"No," she said.

39

"I'm trying to show you how much I love you, Annie. I want to give you a little romance at the same time."

She reluctantly took them. "Fine, but you know I'm not ready to make any commitment."

"I know. It doesn't mean I can't stop trying," Zane replied. "I'll text you when I land."

"Mr. North is making you go to his place in International Falls?"

"Yeah, Minnesota is a lot colder than here. I had to buy new clothes this afternoon. One of the reasons I didn't get a chance to talk to you."

Retying his tie, he eyed her.

"I guess—"

"As much as I would love to stay. I hate to say this, but I have to go now."

This time she kissed him. They hugged for a moment. She tugged and straightened his tie. Then stepped from his arms.

He held out her coat and briefcase. "Remember, only open one card, per day."

She crossed her fingers under her coat. "Okay."

They walked to the building's main front door.

"See you when you get back."

He gave her a quick kiss. "Don't sound so sad. You know I can't handle your pouting. I'll call you."

Not wanting to leave, she hesitated, then pushed open the door. When she reached her car, he still stood at the door watching her.

Their surprising interlude played out in her mind all the way home. When she got there, she immediately took out the three cards from her briefcase.

Each one had her name on the front along with Day Three, Day Four, and Day Five. She contemplated opening them now, but placed them on the kitchen counter and went to take a bath.

Chapter Eleven

The almost three-hour flight to International Falls on Mr. North's private plan didn't go by quickly. Zane sat in the leather chair with nothing to do but think. Mr. North's late night conversation had been close to fairy-taleish.

Zane knew he could be a little offbeat, even eccentric, from time to time.

Snickering, he recalled during his first year as the company's president, he'd seen things that couldn't be justified. There'd been the never-ending supply of inventory. Annie had explained it as standing orders shipped by the vendors.

Then the art department would present new ideals for a toy or paper line and after he'd approve it, the next day shipments would arrive. Mr. North simply indicted he had teams working overtime to get products completed. When he asked where the manufacturing plants were, he never got a straight answer.

As he thought harder, there were Mr. North's unexplained coming and goings, too. Over time he'd learned not to ask questions. Now Mr. North wanted to share—no, fill him in on some proclamation. Was the man terminally ill? Could he be thinking of selling Northern Polar Printing?

Was he going to be fired?

No real answers came.

Soon the usual smell of cookies drew his attention to the stewardess. After a dinner of duck and all the dressing, the stewardess served fresh baked sugar cookies and ice-cold milk. Unable to concentrate, Zane

41

closed his eyes and fell asleep.

"Mr. Ashcroft." A gentle shaking woke him.

Zane's eyelids slowly opened. "Yes?"

"We're preparing to land," the steward said.

"Sorry, must've been the wonderful dinner."

"No, problem," the steward laughed. "You have about ten minutes before you'll have to fasten your seatbelt."

"Thank you."

Zane stood and went to the back of the plane to use the restroom. Reseated, he buckled in and texted Annie.

`Landing soon.`

Amazingly, she replied quickly.

`K. Home.`

Then the plane landed. Waiting on the runway was the signature red limo. The chauffeur, outfitted in a green suit and a red striped tie, held open the door. Mr. North's quirkiness came front and center. Inside the limo was a Christmas wonderland. Jingle bells played. The white leather seats had evergreen shaped pillows scattered on them. Strands of popcorn hung all around the windows.

Smirking, he mused over his childhood belief in Santa until his friends at school ruined the truth. From that point, like everyone else, it was simply a shopping holiday. However now, the spirit of his wonderful indulgence of Christmas pasts haunted him.

"Excuse me, Mr. Ashcroft, we'll be arriving in a few minutes," the chauffeur said over the speaker.

Zane looked out the window as the limo passed two huge stone tree sculptures. The long driveway wound and curved. The sun had set hours ago so he could only make out shadows of tree. After craning his neck, he gave up, and then the privacy window lowered. Through the windshield a massive log house, lit in all white lights came into view.

The limo slowed and came to a stop. The door to his right opened. "Welcome to Mr. North's home," a man in a white suit announced.

"Thank you," Zane replied.

"Please follow me. Mr. North is waiting."

Nodding, Zane took his briefcase and followed the man. Double front doors opened into a great room. A refreshing sent of pine greeted him. Unable to see any Christmas trees or wreaths, he assumed the smell came from an air fresher.

"This way," the man indicated with a sweep of his hand.

Zane was ushered into a room with bookshelves from the ceiling to floor on three of the four walls. An ornate wood desk formed the center point of the back wall. A world globe the size of an exercise ball rested on a pedestal to the right of the desk while a vintage sand hourglass clock sat impressively on the opposite side, also on a pedestal. Zane turned as the door closed and the man left.

In the solitude of the room, he examined the books, tilting his head to read the titles. *The Christmas Carol, Twas The Night Before Christmas*, and books with simply a number on it, eighteen-fifty-nine. The next shelf held the same exact titles, but several books with the number one-thousand-eight-hundred-sixty.

Zane frowned. He went to the next shelf. It repeated the other two, but the number was now one-thousand-eight-hundred-sixty-one. Quickly he scanned all the bookshelves. They all had the same book titles with consecutive numbers. Curiosity won. He took out one numbered one-thousand-nine-hundred-eighty-three and opened it.

The first page read NICE LIST, in all capital letters. The next page was a list of first names and what he assumed were last names. Shutting the book, he examined it more closely. Leather bound with no other marks. He took out a different book with the same number and found it too held names. These started with the letters 'B'. He slid the two books back into their places and went to the very last one. If his suspicions were right, it should be the letter 'Z'.

It was.

Flipping the pages, he found his name, Zane Ashcroft.

"I see you found one of my secrets."

Zane snapped the book closed. "Sorry, I didn't mean—"

Mr. North laughed. Zane thought it sounded more like a ho, ho, ho. Why hadn't he noticed that before now?

"I told you it was time. Sit down, Zane."

He did as he was told; still holding the book numbered one-thousand-nine-hundred-eighty-three, realizing it wasn't a number but a year. Mr. North walked to the other side of the desk and sat. When he did, the world globe lit up and chimed.

"Nineteen-eighty-three was the last year you appeared in my children's NICE LIST books. You, however, reappear in the adult ones in the basement. Zane, I have to go away. You… you need to take over."

Clearing his throat, Zane couldn't decide if he should run to the front door. "Take over, Sir?"

"Yes, my whole operation. Not just the Northern Polar Printing business."

Zane placed the book on the desk and sat up straighter. "I don't understand."

Again, Mr. North laughed and the ho, ho, ho's, were more prominent.

"In time you will, but it's not on our side." Mr. North slid the hourglass front and center. The top bulb was almost empty. "Once the bottom bulb is completely filled, you will…"

Zane listened. His whole insides turned upside down. Logic and reason held no meaning.

Chapter Twelve

After a few hours of twisting and turning in bed, Annie put on her blue robe and went to the kitchen. She stared at the cards on the counter. The microwave clock indicated it was five minutes after twelve.

Tearing open Day Three, a sense a naughtiness struck her. Her promise gone. An illustration of, The Christmas Carol famous three ghosts, the past, present, and future was on the front. Opening it she read his message—

Our future is nothing without our past, I love you.

She read it again and again. The tears fell and she didn't try to stop them.

Damn him, he was right.

Without an argument or disagreement in a relationship there wasn't a future. The Day Four card beckoned to her. She opened it.

A beautiful sketch of a four-story house, nestled in the woods, was on the front. Opening it, she read the message.

Our next home? Miss you,
Love Zane.

The man had a romantic side she hadn't anticipated. Drumming her fingers on the counter, she pushed Day Five away. Turning off the lights,

45

she headed up the stairs. She only made it half-way before turning around and hurrying back to the kitchen. She slid her finger under the lip of the last envelope and took out the card.

Five golden rings sparkled. Inhaling sharply, she read the message—

I'll marry you any day,
Love, Zane.

This time, she went up the stairs holding the card to her chest. She placed it under her pillow. A scent of cookies wafted through the air. She fell asleep quickly.

In dreamland, she and Zane were visiting a town made to look like Santa's home in the North Pole. Zane wore an elaborate Santa suit. Oddly, he had a short beard and it wasn't white. He talked to deer as she spoke to people dressed in elf outfits.

Everyone was cheery and bright including her own skin-tight, floor-length red dress. She wore a white apron with the top folded over. The elf people scurried around so fast they were a blur.

So carried away by her dream, she felt it was real when Zane glanced over at her and winked.

* * * *

Awaking to the alarm clock, Annie sat upright.

She was in her own bed, not in an old-fashioned hotel in the middle of nowhere. Shutting off the alarm, she took card Day Five out from under her pillow. Lifting it, she inhaled.

No cookie smell.

She frowned in confusion, dismissing the weirdness of her dream. Shoving off the warmth of the comforter, she began her morning routine.

When she arrived at work, she'd placed all the opened cards in her drawer. She'd just taken her seat after checking on the day's shipments when her phone rang.

"Hello, Ms. McGrath."

"Good morning, sweetheart."

"Zane," she breathed into the phone.

"The one and only. I have a busy schedule today and wanted to touch base with you before the day got away from me."

She caught herself as he talked, unwilling to let him know she'd read all the cards. "Mr. Elfner said everything is running smoothly. The IT department has been double and triple checking the computers and connections."

"Good, I saw we had an unusual heavy ordering night. It's okay for you to authorize overtime if needed."

"I don't think we will, but I'll let Mr. Elfner know..." She paused. "I want to say—"

"Annie, stop. You have nothing to apologize for. It's me who should. Apparently you read card three. Loving someone as much as I love you is new to me. We're meant to be together through the rough and good times. I'm sorry I'm not there in person to tell you and show you."

Annie waved her hand in front of her face as a fan, to dry the tears that threatened. "Zane—"

"Gotta go. Text me later."

"Okay," she gasped.

Then he was gone. She held the phone in a daze.

What was wrong with her? She didn't cry.

"You're too young for hot flashes." Clarice stood at her office doorway.

Annie tilted her head and replaced the phone. "Is it time for our morning meeting?"

"In a bit. Did you want me to get the conference room?"

"That'll be fine. Have Nick set out orange juice with the bagels and donuts," Annie replied.

"Gotcha, see yeah in five."

Clarice left and Annie took out the Day Three Card.

What was their past? Five years of knowing each other. Sex in his office on nights they stayed late. Moving on to overnight at each other homes. The fun and newness of a relationship.

What was their present? Fighting? Mistrust? Sex only so often. Living for the moment. Had they become complacent?

Then, what would their future be? Marriage? Children? She was too old to have kids. Did Zane even want any? They'd never discussed it, but

47

adoption was something to consider. What if one of them moved to a different company?

Her head hurt from all the possibilities and unknowns.

"Ms. McGrath, you're wanted in the conference room."

Startled, Annie rose from her chair at the announcement over the intercom. Crap! She hurried to her meeting with no answers.

* * * *

The remainder of the third day and the entire fourth day went by fast. She'd covered up the fact she'd opened all of the cards the first night by texting Zane on day four at one-o'clock with an emoji smiling face heart. He in return called her at two o'clock. They chatted for only a few minutes. Nether speaking of their argument.

The fifth day was the longest. The Day Five Card's five's rings and message would be hard not to discuss. Foregoing a one o'clock text as an inadequate way to reply, she waited for him.

Right at two o'clock he called.

"I hope Card Five didn't upset you," Zane started. "I mean it, Annie. I'll marry you any day."

"If that's your way of a proposal—"

"Oh Annie, you're so funny. Trust me when I do, and I do intend to, I'll be there in person."

She shifted in her chair. "Okay, let's move onto a different topic."

"I love you. You keep me grounded, Annie. Hold on."

She heard him through what seemed like a covering of the phone. "Santa will be…. No, I'm…" There was a muffled reply by someone and then static.

"Sorry about that. One of Mr. North's employee's needs me to read a contract. I'll try to get out of here in a couple of hours. I really miss you."

"I miss you too. You better take care of that contract."

They said goodbye.

She waited the rest of the afternoon for an update and it came at six p.m. via a text.

        Still in MN. Arriving late. See U in

48

`the morning.`

Her anticipation went from one hundred to zero.

`I'll keep the bed warm for U.`

His response.

`Nice. You'll need your beauty sleep. Don't wait up.`

Annie paused, then sent her reply, an emoji smiley face with wide-open eyes and a coffee cup.

`Go home.` (It included a bed with an emoji.) `LOL.`

Laughing, she packed up and headed home not wanting to believe, he wouldn't come over to her house. She'd stayed up past midnight expecting him to appear. When it was clear he wasn't coming, she went to bed.

With eagerness of a teenager, day six arrived. She took special care with her hair and makeup, forgetting their argument as she selected her outfit.

Once at work, an adrenaline rush coursed through her at the sight of his car. She parked and nearly ran inside. A light shone in his office. Every ounce of her wanted to go to him. Did she want to be the cat or mouse? His shadow spilled into the hallway and the mouse won. She flipped on the lights in her office and smiled.

There on her desk with a coffee was the Day Six Card. She had to give him credit for being so thoughtful. Her heart raced. Ignoring the drink, she opened the card.

A picturesque scene of a mother goose with six babies swimming in a lake covered the front. Inside was a handwritten message.

I'm sorry. I'm waiting for your approval to

return to your bed to make love to you. Tonight?
Love, Zane.

Annie felt his presence and looked up from the card. He was a welcome sight. Had it only been four days since she'd last seen him? It felt like weeks. No months.

"You're here early," she managed to say.

"The perks of a private jet and being the president," Zane replied.

"How was your meeting with Mr. North?"

"Very enlightening to say the least. He has a beautiful home. Quite large as a matter of fact, nothing like I expected. He said the next time you're to come with me."

"Really? Interesting, and when will that be?"

"After we get married."

"Shhhh, I told you I didn't want to get married," Annie said. "It'll only ruin what we have."

"Have dinner with me."

She walked around her desk and sat behind it. "I suppose. You pick the place."

"Is that a yes to my question on the card, too?"

His irresistible smile wasn't a force to combat. "Time will tell. Let me know what time tonight. Now go, I've work to do."

"That's my Annie, all business. Six-thirty. We'll go in my car."

Before she could respond he was gone.

The morning passed slowly. Her heart pounded every time she heard his voice in the hallway. Noon came and went much the same as the morning. When employees began to say goodnight, she went to the bathroom with her emergency kit. Freshening her makeup, she unbuttoned an extra button to show off her cleavage and the lacy bra she wore. As she went through the general office area not a single employee remained. Back in her office, she paced.

"Ready?"

In mid-stride she stopped, pivoting to face Zane. "I am."

They stopped by the security desk. "Rudy, we'll be leaving Ms.

McGrath's car overnight."

"Hopefully we won't get any snow. The plow trucks don't like it when there are cars in the parking lot," Rudy said.

"Here are my keys in case it does. You can have it moved," Annie said.

"Let me check the radar on my weather app." Rudy swiped and tapped at his phone. "Good news. No winter storms. I'll inform the night guard when he comes in at eight."

"Thanks." Annie pocketed her keys.

"Have a goodnight," Zane said and put his hand the small of her back.

They briskly walked to his car. Again, he'd use the remote start, making the inside toasty warm.

When he merged onto Highway 176, Annie broke the silence. "I loved each of the cards," she paused. "I've forgiven you, but I hope you'll be able to share important news and decisions with me in the future."

He reached over and took her gloved hand. In the darkness of the car, she stared longingly at him. The black cloud that had been hanging over their relationship vanished, replaced by a storm of intoxicating waves of desire.

"Mr. North wanted me to tell you he was sorry he hadn't included you. The merger was hit and miss for a while. When it happened, it was so fast. I only found out minutes before the meeting."

Annie sighed in relief. The old school saying about never going to bed mad must've come from a woman.

"I over reacted, we can move on. Enough of business, where are you taking me for dinner?"

"Kyoto's," Zane announced.

Her stomach rumbled at the thought of the Japanese steakhouse.

Chapter Thirteen

Zane watched Annie closely during dinner. His three-day absence from her intensified his love for her. He struggled to be a gentleman, only allowing himself minimal touching. As they concluded dinner, the owners stopped at their table to wish them a Merry Christmas.

Outside, Zane opened the passenger's side door for her and decided it was time for the gentleman to leave.

He kissed her. The light touching of their lips became more. One kiss led to a second and then a third. The smooth leather of her gloved hand on his neck encouraged him. He coaxed her mouth open deepening the kiss. Now both her gloved hands were on his neck, sliding to the back and up into his hair. She leaned into him.

"I missed you," he crooned.

"I did, too."

She ran her hand over his lips in a caress, and then got into the car. Stilling his racing pulse, he walked around the car. The ten-minute ride was done in silence. Her outside timed light helped as he steered into her driveway. He parked, contemplating whether she'd invite him in.

"I had a wonderful time on our dinner date," he said.

"It's been a while since we'd gone out on the spur of the moment."

"Sorry about that, I'll try harder not to let business get in our way again. What time should I pick you up in the morning?"

She shifted in the passenger's seat to face him. "The answer to today's card is—" She smiled, leaned over, and kissed him. "Yes."

Zane cradled her head with his hands and kissed her back. "Here? In the car?"

She laughed, opened the car door, and ran for the house. Quickly he followed to the front door. Inside she'd already kicked off her high heels shoes, her coat fell to the floor, and she headed up the stairs. Her single glance over her shoulder was all it took.

Shoeless too, he clambered up the stairs two and three at a time to meet her in the bedroom. Annie had her skirt off, flaunting a red garter belt with no underwear. He inhaled sharply. She was going to be the death of him. Her sensuality was off the charts. Discarding his suit jacket, he emptied the space between them and brushed her hands away from the buttons of her blouse. For the first time in his life his hands trembled as he slipped each button through the buttonholes.

Her breath softly caressed his cheek. Her hands unhooked and unzipped his pants, and cupped his shaft.

"Take me now." Her request wasn't a request; it was a demand.

He was more than happy to do her bidding. Zane backed her up against the pole of the four-poster bed. She lifted her leg, placing her foot on the footboard.

The view was overwhelming sexy. He tugged his pants and boxers down, kicking them across the room. Annie hugged the pole behind her.

"You're being very naughty," he breathed hoarsely.

Her tongue licked her lips. He replied by cupping both her breasts, freeing them from a matching red lacy bra. Suckling the right mound then moving to the other. Her moans of pleasure echoed in the room. With one hand he guided himself into her softness. She flung her head back, still holding tight to the pole.

"Let go, Annie."

Her arms wound around his neck as he lifted her. Her legs encircled his waist as he moved in and out. The awkward position lasted only for a second and the bed became their playground. She removed her lace bra while he returned to her fully naked.

Zane ran his hands over the silkiness of the nylons still attached to the garters. Her hand cased his bare chest. Neither needed nor wanted too much foreplay. Their desire was beyond careful intimacy. He plunged into her heat. Annie's cry of pleasure broke the little restraint he'd been holding to as her body melted. Pushing deeper to find the spot he knew would be her release.

53

"Yes, yes, yes." she pleaded.

He kissed her when the tremors consumed her. Before the last spasm, he peaked and yielded to his own release as the liquid fire poured into her.

Their heavy breathing slowed and he leaned on his arm, to look at Annie. "I love you."

Her eyes remained closed, but her lips curved into a smile and she nestled closer.

Chapter Fourteen

A buzzing sound interrupted Annie's sleep. She tapped at the alarm clock on the nightstand. Failing to make the annoying noise stop, she sat up. Rubbing sleep from her eyes, she canceled the alarm.

"Zane, time to—"

The area next to her was empty and cold to the touch, but a card lay on the pillow. Before she was able to reach for it, her cell phone rang. Zane's picture appeared as the caller ID.

Tapping accept and before she could say hello, he did. "Good morning, sweetheart. I'll be there in an hour."

"You left?"

"I did. Still giving you your space. You haven't formally invited me back to your home."

Shoving off the blanket, Annie rose. "Okay, I'll be ready." She paused. "I love you."

The line went quiet.

"Hello?"

"I'm here. It's good to hear the words from you. Don't forget to open the Day Seven Card. See you soon."

"But—"

The call ended. After hurrying into the bathroom, she took a shower and got ready. Forty-five minutes later dressed and the bed made, she retrieved the card.

Her coat had been hung up and she grinned, recalling their spontaneous lovemaking. Tucking the card into her pocket, she waited for Zane. A spray of headlights lights lit the hallway as he pulled into her

55

driveway. The sun hadn't risen yet, leaving everything dull and dark. Once she buckled in, she saw he held a Starbucks coffee.

"I told you I've forgiven you."

"I know, but it won't stop me from being the caring other half," Zane remarked.

She took the coffee and sipped. "Mmmm. What's the blend?"

"Christmas. I hoped it wouldn't be too strong."

"It isn't, thanks."

The morning drive was the same as it usually was before their fight, quiet. A few blocks from the office Zane's phone rang.

He clicked the talk button on the steering wheel. "Hello?"

She saw Mr. North name appear on the dash.

"Good morning, Zane. I hope your return flight went smoothly."

"Yes, it did. I have Annie in the car with me, and you're on speaker."

"Great. Good morning, Ms. McGrath."

"Good morning, Mr. North," she replied.

"I'm sorry about this, but Zane I need you to return to International Falls for a few days."

Annie exhaled and looked out the side window.

"I can be ready in a few hours," Zane replied.

"I'll have the limo pick you up by three o'clock. Annie, I promise to have him home in time for the company's Christmas party."

"No worries, Mr. North," she responded.

"I do believe that was a little white lie," Mr. North scolded.

Zane struggled to hold his laughter. Annie punched him in the arm.

"No, you're right," she said. She raised her eyebrows as she stared at Zane who only shrugged his shoulders.

"Santa is going to be very nice to you this Christmas, Annie." The lined crackled, then Mr. North continued. "Zane, Mr. Moonracer will be joining us, too."

"Sounds great. Anything you need me to bring?"

"Nothing I can think of. If we do, Annie should be able to email us the necessary papers. Okay, thanks, see you tonight."

"Yes, bye."

"Goodbye, Mr. North," Annie chimed in just as they arrived at work.

The call ended. Zane drummed his fingers on the steering wheel. Quietness filled the car. The engine hummed. She turned toward him.

"Sorry, I wanted to—"

"Don't, it will only be three more days, four at the most."

"I'll have to drive back home to pack. Want me to pick up something for lunch?"

"Surprise me."

Zane kissed her, and then before she could pull away he kissed her again. This one was a battle of their tongues. His hand reached inside of her coat cupping her right breast. Her blouse came unbuttoned allowing him to free her aching breast. She covered his hand with hers.

"Zane, stop. Or I'll make you take me with you back to your house."

Their foreheads met. "You're right. I'm being greedy. Don't forget to open the Day Seven Card if you haven't already."

Fixing her bra and blouse, she nodded, leaned in, and gave him a quick kiss. "Don't forget my lunch."

"I won't."

She opened the car door and walked to the building. Clarice was waiting for her when she entered her office.

"Annie, you've got to see this."

"Let me get my coat off."

"I can talk while you're doing that," Clarice declared, waving papers.

"Holly Blitzen from the Hyatt emailed pics of the table decorations and the specs of the room. I'm keeping these for my own new ideas file. Can we go over there to see them?"

With the Day Seven Card in her hand, Annie sat. Clarice placed the papers in front of her. She set the card to the side, giving her attention to the pictures. The hotel was allowing them their choice of small real Christmas trees, carved wooden reindeer, or miniature gingerbread houses.

"Oh, and by the way, Nick was here to see you this morning."

"He was?" Annie frowned.

"Yeah, I saw him come out of your office and I asked him if I could help him."

"Thank you. I'm sure if it was important, he'll come by again." Annie shivered in spite of the warmth of the room. "No, we can't go over to the Hyatt. Why does Northern Polar Printing Company think it's nice to have a Holiday Party off-site? I wish we would have it here."

Once the words she spoke, she regretted her candor. For six years she'd enjoyed the Christmas parties at the Hyatt Regency O'Hare Hotel even though she disagreed with the cost.

"Stop being the Grinch. Wipe that scowl from your face. The Hyatt has been a great place to host our corporate party. It's so nice the company gives each employee a one-night stay. I'm thinking of upgrading my room. I don't care why it's done this way," Clarice professed.

Annie smiled and shook her head. Clarice had missed her calling. Her romantic side always slipped into her everyday ho-hum routine. If she was to make a go of the party planning business, she'd need that element to be successful.

"It's done for liability purposes. So no one drives home intoxicated. Why couldn't we be like other companies and have an afternoon lunch for all their employees? No, we're different." Annie sipped the last of her coffee.

"You've been real secretive since the meeting. How are things with you and the Pres?"

"Like it's any of your business."

"Oh that hurt," Clarice groaned. "Must be better. You have a certain glow to your face this morning."

Picking up the card, she smiled. "He's been giving me a card every day with a number on it. Today is seven. It's weird, but fun."

Clarice was silent for a minute. "Hey, that's like The Twelve Days of Christmas, but we're too early for the days to work out. Every year my mom does fun things for the twelve days. Day One doesn't start for another five days. Well, aren't you going to open it?"

Annie agreed, it seemed like the twelve days of something. "Okay."

The card featured an old fashion number seven and the word anniversary on the front. She frowned. It wasn't their anniversary. They've dated four years and for that matter, only known each other for five. Inside, was a verse.

58

You're my life.
You make me happy every day.
Seven days a week, I am your slave.
Just like the first day I met you to
yesterday.

Then Zane had added a handwritten note to the bottom of the card.

I know it's not our anniversary, but it was
the only card I found with the number seven
on it.
I love you, Zane.

"Are you going to share or not?"

"As a matter of fact, no. I will tell you it's very romantic."

"You're the luckiest woman on earth. Let me know if you change your mind about a field trip," Clarice said as she left.

Annie placed the card in the drawer with the other six. What was the significance of the cards and numbers? Clarice had brought up a good point. She counted the days to twelve. It landed on the day of the company's Christmas party. The puzzle was unnerving. A warning voice reminded her of card five's marriage proposal possibility. Hating to admit it, she was secretly excited at the idea and a hundred percent scared at the same time. Her automatic non-committal attitude kicked in, reminding her, she didn't need to marry to find happiness.

Chapter Fifteen

Throwing dirty clothes into the hamper, Zane repacked his suitcase. Mr. North's unexpected request to return to International Falls was inconvenient. With only five days before his pending life-changing question for Annie, he wouldn't be able to oversee all the details. From his dresser, he took the Day Eight, Nine, Ten, and Eleven Cards, tucking them in his suit's inside breast pocket.

Locking his house, he drove back to the office and made a detour to the grocery store, Dominick's, for his and Annie's lunch. His need to see her was unbearable. Never had a woman gotten under his skin like she had. He wanted her by his side every hour of every day. He'd given her the space she'd demanded by not staying the night. It had been hard to leave her warm soft body before she woke.

The sun had come out, melting the last day's snow. The Northern Polar Printing building took on a different look in the sunlight. It appeared invisible with all the glass windows reflecting the sun. Zane walked inside.

"Good morning... uh, good afternoon, Suzy."

"Oh, Mr. Ashcroft, good afternoon to you too. Sammie gave me your itinerary. She went to lunch." She held out an envelope.

"Thank you," he responded and accepted it.

Not wasting any more time, he went to Annie's office. She sat at her desk, reading papers. He momentarily let his gaze caress her face.

"I have lunch if you're hungry."

Annie looked up, brushing a wayward strand of hair from her eyes. "I am. You made good time. We can eat at my desk."

60

He closed the door. "Caesar salad and breadsticks, no tip necessary."

She moved papers aside to make room. "You know the way to a woman's heart. I see you take being a slave seriously."

He set the bag on her desk and took out the two to-go-boxes. "You read the card?"

"I did. It was very touching. Too bad I won't be able to take advantage of your new status," Annie said sweetly with a smile.

"Wow. It's getting warm in here." He pulled the chair closer to her desk. Before sitting, he took off his outercoat, laying it over the back. Reaching into his suit jacket, he withdrew the cards. "I brought days eight through eleven."

"Are you going to tell me what the meaning is behind the numbers and the cards?"

He placed them on her desk and sat. "You just have to wait and see."

The conversation from then on entailed the company's end of year figures and what each employee's bonuses was to be.

"Zane, these are a lot higher then I budgeted for the year," Annie protested.

"Mr. North wants to make this Christmas special."

"It most definitely will with these amounts."

"I hate to eat and run." He studied her, trying to read her reaction and mood. Missing her already, he hadn't even left yet. He lingered, pacing the room.

What if after all his plans, she turned him down? Abruptly he sat back down and seized her hands, holding them tight.

"Zane, what's wrong?"

"Nothing—I don't want to ruin my surprise, but I'm not one to—"

"If, you're talking about the possibility of a proposal. I told you we don't need to get married. We're too old to care what other people think."

"It matters to me, Annie." Zane lifted her hands and kissed her fingertips. "I'll be asking you to marry me at the party. I wanted it to be spontaneous but I know you hate surprises. This will give you time to get used to the idea."

He released her hands and tapped the stack of cards. "Remember,

61

only open one a day."

"That's so unfair. You know I have no patience."

Before he did something stupid, he got to his feet. Clenching his jaw, he gave her a half smile, opened the door, and left. Annie called his name, but he refused to look at her.

Even though for the most part, they'd technically made up, he still wanted to give her space. The possibility of marriage was something neither of them took lightly.

Checking his watch, he realized he had a half hour before the limo would arrive. Instead of going to his office, he went out to the security guards station. Rudy sat at the desk scanning the monitors.

"Good afternoon, Mr. O'Deere."

"Good afternoon, Mr. Ashcroft." Rudy stopped what he was doing and straightened. "Is there something I can do for you?"

"Yes, as a matter fact, there is. I have to leave again for several days, and I have some concerns about an employee."

Rudy stood and motioned for him to come into the security office. Inside, Zane glanced at another set of monitors. It never failed to impress him how the N & N Security Company had all the new and innovative technology.

Zane took a deep breath. "Can you send me a daily email with Mr. Pole's in and out punches, plus if you see him entering Ms. McGrath's or my office?"

"Of course. I'll have to adjust some of the cameras. Is there something special you want me to be on the lookout for?"

"No, no, no. I'm sure it's nothing. Just make sure I get those emails. Thanks for your time." Zane left the room.

He'd barely completed a few calls and printouts when Suzy announced the limo was waiting. On his way out, he stopped by Annie's office but she wasn't there.

Inside the limo he texted her.

```
On my way.
```

About to board Mr. North's plane her reply came with an emoji smiley face with hearts. Mentally measuring his options, caution won and he sent a matching emoji.

When the plane reached cruising altitude, the smell of cookies hit him. The whirlwind of the last few days still fresh, he struggled to comprehend all Mr. North had shared. Taking out the inventory file, he tried to redirect his thoughts, but fell asleep.

"Mr. Ashcraft. Excuse me, we'll be landing soon."

Zane jerked awake and stared at the flight attendant. "Thank you."

He'd been dreaming of a sleigh with reindeer. He was the person in a Santa suit yelling at them to fly away.

Where had the two and a half hours gone? Stretching, he wondered why this plane made him fall asleep? Shoving the file into his briefcase, he prepared for the descent.

Like the last time, a red limo waited with the same chauffeur in a green suit. However, tonight the song playing on the audio system was "Rudolph the Red Nose Reindeer." Snickering, Zane made himself comfortable for the half-hour drive.

At the headquarters building, the butler, as Zane named the man in the white suit, ushered him into Mr. North's office, but this time, Mr. Moonracer was waiting along with Mr. North.

"Come sit down, Zane," Mr. North requested.

Zane gave his coat to the butler and sat in the chair next to Mr. Moonracer. "Good evening, gentlemen."

"I'm sure you're hungry, but first we wanted to show you our entire operation. It's also about time you started calling me Chris," Mr. North said with a rumbling throaty laugh. Just then, the big world globe lit up and chimed six times. "Goodness, more added to the Nice List."

Mr. Moonracer combed his fingers through his beard. "Better than the naughty."

Zane inhaled deeply, eyeing the two men and wondering if this was some sort of prank.

63

Chapter Sixteen

Ready to call it a day, Annie placed all four cards in front of her. Hesitantly, she picked up the one-labeled Eight. She twirled it around, and then placed it back in order. She wanted badly to open them all up, as she had before.

"Night, Annie," Clarice said.

Annie looked up and pushed all the cards together. "I'm heading out, too. If you wait a minute, we can walk together."

"That's okay. I parked out by the warehouse."

Smiling, Annie understood Clarice's meaning. "Well, then I guess I'll see you in the morning."

"Right. Have a good night," Clarice replied.

Scooping up the cards, Annie leaned down to stick them into her briefcase. When she straightened she caught a movement out of the corner of her eye.

"Clarice?"

Annie listened but heard no reply. Gathering her things, she walked out of her office. To her right she glimpsed Nick hurrying down the corridor. With no one else around, she didn't want a confrontation. She hurried to the parking lot and to her car.

As she backed out, she saw Nick in the rearview mirror, standing in the receptionist area watching her. His leering stare, horribly creepy, was intensified by the darkness. Steering the car, she put it into drive. When she looked over at the building, he was gone. Mentally she reminded herself to talk to N & N Security to run a check of him.

Instead of going straight home, she headed over to the Woodfield

Mall. She'd put off dress shopping long enough. Her phone rang as she made a left turn onto Hwy 14. The console showed it was Zane.

"Hello," she said.

"I've landed and am on my way to Mr. North's home. It's freezing up here."

"It isn't much warmer here," Annie responded and clicked on the seat warmer.

"Are you on your way home?"

"Nope, I'm going shopping. A girl has to have something to do when her man is unavailable."

"Use my credit card. Get anything you want."

His generous offer was exciting. She never let him buy her anything, but then a thought crossed her mind. "Well, I could stop by Victoria's Secret."

"Wow! You're being heartless. Just the thought of you in the garter belt last night is tempting me to tell the driver to turn around so I can come home."

She laughed and stopped at the Woodfield Mall entrance intersection. "Now who's being naughty?"

They talked for few more minutes with him promising to call in the morning. After using the valet parking for convenience, she entered the crowded mall. To some people it would've been a turn off, but to her it was invigorating, from the holiday music to the families waiting in line for their chance to see Santa.

As she walked by the visit Santa area, she had to look twice at the man sitting in the huge golden chair. At first, she thought he looked like Mr. North. Frowning at her own stupidity, she told herself it couldn't be the owner of Northern Polar Printing because Zane was meeting with him any minute. However, she moved to get a better view. The Santa could've been Mr. North's twin. The man nodded in her direction before scooping up a little girl waiting to sit on his lap. Then her view was blocked again. Dismissing her uncertainties, she blamed it on the Christmas spirit, holiday decorations, and the carols.

Even with all the shoppers, Annie was energized. The merriment was an aphrodisiac. She went from store to store in her search for a special holiday dress. About to give up, she took a group of dresses into the fitting room. When she tried on the last one, she knew she'd found the perfect one.

The gold, slim fitted, knee-length sequined dress with pearl like beads had a plunging neckline and off the shoulder cap sleeves. It looked stunning on her. Excited now, she searched for shoes and then to complete the outfit, swung into Victoria's Secret for special undergarments.

Arriving home with an armful of packages and more in the car, she wasn't tired. The Christmas spirit remained with her. She made a cup of expresso and then began bringing up boxes and tubs from the basement. It was time to decorate her house. After a third cup of coffee, she turned on Christmas music from the Sirius XM mobile app. By midnight she decided to call it night and open the Day Eight Card.

Her promise to not open them until the specific day abandoned as she tore open the Day Eight Card. She stared at a picture of a nighttime blue sky along with a sleigh and reindeer on top of a roof. Inside she read Zane's message.

Mr. North reminded me about the Christmas magic. I hope you remember it, too. I'd ask you out for dinner again, but since I'm gone, dream of me naked in your bed.
Love, Zane.

Standing the card up on the counter, she opened the next card. Nine old fashion carolers greeted her.

"Oh my," she exclaimed aloud.

I know a spot that makes you sing,
Zane.

She fanned herself. The intimate place did indeed make her scream and an image of him doing it made her squirm. Setting it next to the other card, she grabbed the Day Ten Card, anxious to read his message.

A box of ten chocolates adorned the front.

I miss your morning kisses and our never-ending goodnight kisses.

Tears welled up. How could she have been so wrong about him? She'd let their professional life get between their private relationship life.

The last card, Day Eleven, laid in front of her. Her pride battled her inner turmoil. Past the point of no return, her heart pounded. Reaching for the last one, she carefully slid the card from the envelope. No picture was on the front only words,

11 Reasons why I love you.

She hesitated for a second and then opened it. One single sentence was repeated eleven times.

Because you're you.

Annie sank to the floor crying. How could she not want to marry him?

Chapter Seventeen

Determined to stay awake on the return flight home, Zane asked for coffee. The last four days passed in a blur of unbelievable information. Mr. North—Chris had shared his success and the reality of Christmas. Even now, as Zane sat on the plane, he doubted the world would ever be able to accept that Santa was real. He even struggled with the mystical revelation. It was a masterfully hidden truth over the centuries.

Zane had no idea how Annie would take it. They'd talked several times during his time in International Falls. He'd kept business separate when he'd call to just talk to her. She admitted the first day; she hadn't waited to open the cards. He'd expected she wouldn't. Each of his messages, he'd tried to tell her how he loved her.

Checking the time, he debated if he should go and see her after landing. As much as he wanted to see her and make love to her, the morning would have to be good enough. Instead, he texted her.

```
In route. Arrive after midnight. See u
in the morning at work. I'll bring the
coffee.
```

An extra benefit of flying on a private jet, the use of WIFI, calls, and the ability to text. He could get used to this luxury.

```
Are you sure? I'll wait for u.
```

Tempting as it was he declined.

```
We'll have time tomorrow night after
the party.
```

He added a kiss emoji.

```
Can't wait.
```

(Along with two lines of kiss emoji's.)

He took his last card, Day Twelve, from his briefcase. A simple blank card. His idea was, to not have anything influence her answer when he proposed. The stewardess brought the requested coffee with a plate of bell shaped sugar cookies.

Scratching his chin, with a day growth of beard. He wondered how he'd missed all the subtle hints. It was as if he was seeing things for the first time. He knew he'd put aside all the Christmas references from Mr. North as being eccentric. Sipping the coffee, the caffeine soon took effect. He thought hard for a message to Annie.

She was the love of his life. Without her, he felt shockingly void. Without her, he wasn't whole.

How did he put that into words? A new set of improbabilities washed over him. What would her reaction be to the news about Chris? How would the new position he was sworn to uphold affect their relationship? Mr. North had been adamant that once he and Annie married, they'd take over all aspects of the businesses completely.

Scowling, he chose his word carefully and wrote.

Annie,
I love you! I want us to be together always.
Tonight, you'll have the last word. I hope
with all my heart you'll say, yes.
Yours forever, Zane.

Rereading the words, his heart soared. He'd never believed feeling about a woman this way was possible. Then the dreaded doubt seeped into his thoughts. What if she said no? It was a possibility he couldn't dwell upon.

Chris had said not to worry and that all things would fall into place. The sand hourglass had almost emptied into the bottom globe showing time wasn't a friend at the moment. Mr. Moonracer and Chris had also said they didn't have time to complete everything. He'd assured both men that he and Annie would indeed get married.

"Mr. Ashcroft, Mr. North is on the red phone."

Red phone? He'd never seen any phones on the plane besides cell phones. The steward pressed a button on the front of the armrest. A red phone appeared. He raised it.

"Hello?"

"Zane, we have a disturbing chain of events that might occur…"

He listened in disbelief that what was happening was absolutely real. It had to be the damn cookie smell.

Chapter Eighteen

Annie drummed her fingers on her cell phone. Having been unable to sleep, she'd given up and went into work early to wait for Zane. Checking the time, the clock read ten after seven. She'd been waiting for only thirty minutes. Zane still hadn't appeared. Hearing a noise outside her office, she got up and walked around her desk.

Before making it to the doorway, the love of her life appeared, still wearing his overcoat and holding two cups of coffee. He took her breath away.

"Good morning, Annie."

His tone said it all, deep and sensuous. A few steps took her in front of him, breathing in his scent. Reaching up, she ran her hands over his five-o'clock shadow. The whiskers pricking her palms sent her pulse racing. Desire overwhelmed her.

"I like the new look," she whispered.

Her lips gently touched his and then she hugged him, uncaring if employees were watching.

"Let me set down the coffees."

"Sorry. I can't believe you're here. I had visions of you calling to say Mr. North was keeping you a few more days."

He laughed as she moved away to allow him to enter her office.

"No way would I miss tonight. You know I love playing Santa."

"Right. Here I thought it was because you missed me." She pouted and crossed her arms in front of her.

Once he put their coffees down, he handed her the Day Twelve

71

Card. The air glimmered with undercurrents of a different kind. Gone was the excitement and playfulness.

"This is my final one. I'll be in and out all day and wanted to make sure I gave it to you in person."

"Zane, please don't give me an ultimatum."

"You are not an ultimatum."

"I didn't mean it that way. Let's not talk about this right now," she said. Taking the card, she put it in her desk drawer with the other eleven.

"I didn't want to bother you when you were with Mr. North, but Nick has been acting very weird the last few days. He scares me." Annie took a file from her in-basket and held it out to him. "Here's a log of my complaints and a list of other possibilities for a janitorial service."

He accepted the file and picked up his coffee. "I'll look it over, but I'm telling you, there is nothing to be afraid of."

"Are you saying that as the president because you have to, or as my… my lover."

"That isn't fair, Annie." He brushed his hand through his hair and then tapped the file against his other hand before walking to her doorway. "Don't worry I'll take care of this."

"Right! We've come full circle again. An impasse over an employee. Business verses personal life." Why did her concerns fall on deaf ears with him?

Now wasn't the time to push the issue, she reminded herself. "Thanks for the coffee. When you have time, I'd like to discuss some figures with you before I print the bonus checks for tonight," she said.

"Call when you're ready. Don't forget to open your card."

Then he was gone.

She took a hesitant step to follow him, but turned around and sat down. Their meeting hadn't gone as she'd imagined. Her excitement of seeing him had been real while his standoffish attitude had been a surprise.

Annie scolded herself. For heaven's sake we work to together. We can't be a couple twenty-four-seven.

She had to take measures to keep their private life from the office atmosphere. The eagerness from eleven days ago to open each card turned into apprehension. Opening the drawer, she snatched the last card.

72

Stroking it, a smell of sugar cookies drifted to her. With care, she opened it.

Puzzlement set in. No picture to look at. No words to read on the front, however, inside each letter of every word Zane had written spoke of devotion. He'd hinted at a coming proposal.

Her stomached cramped. How would she respond tonight? If she were to say no, she knew she'd lose him forever. Their non-committal relationship had moved to the next level without her approval.

If, she said yes, could they work together as husband and wife? Few couples could make a go of it, each trying to be the more dominant. Was she willing to take the low road for love?

"Happy Holiday Party Day, Annie."

She looked up. Clarice held a tray of what seemed to be peanut butter kiss cookies and a gift bag.

Damn, she forgot today was the pre-party celebration. "Are they homemade?"

"They are. I brought in extra in case you forgot yours to share."

"You're heaven sent, Clarice. It skipped my mind. Is that your Secret Santa gift?"

"Oh—what gift?"

"The one you're holding."

Annie watched Clarice who was clearly uneasy. She shifted the plate of cookies to one hand to the other hand holding the bag went to her side. In what appeared as an act to hide it.

"Yup, Secret Santa gift. I'll be back and start running the bonus checks."

Choosing not to pursue it further, she realized it might be for her or Rudy. Annie replaced the card on top of the others in the drawer, then rose.

"I don't have them ready yet. I'll go talk to Zane right now."

"Okay, see you in a few."

From the file cabinet, Annie lifted the one labeled, Bonus Checks, and walked passed a stunned Clarice. When she entered his office, Zane sat his desk going through mail.

"Do you have time to go over the numbers for the checks?"

Without looking up. "Always for you," he said, staring at

73

something. "I went over your concerns about Nick. I have N & N Security running a full background check."

She sat in the chair in front of him. Relief flooded through her. She let his comment slide for the time being and for the next twenty minutes they discussed the figures for the bonus checks.

"It means a lot to me, that you're backing me about Nick."

"It has nothing to do with believing. You brought up valid concerns."

Her earlier relief vanished, replaced by rage. Abruptly standing, she walked out.

"Annie, wait," he called.

She didn't stop. No one acknowledged her, as she hurried past them, escaping to the bathroom. Inside one of the stalls she forced back her tears.

How could he treat her this way? How could she say yes to him?

Pacing the cramped space of the area, she tried to figure out why Zane was being so cold toward her. For a man who proclaimed he loved her, he didn't act like it. Shoving her hands into her suit jacket pockets she felt something in the left one. Taking out the object, she stared at an old unopened fortune cookie. She remembered then about six months ago when Mr. North had taken all of the directors to PF Chang for lunch. All the employees laughed at their fortune cookies words of advice. She'd slipped hers into her pocket, not wanting to read it.

She tugged the plastic open and broke the cookie, unfolding the strip of paper. "Magic is real. So is love."

"Stupid. I hate these things," she murmured. Throwing it into the toilet, she flushed it away.

Calmer, she made her way back to her office, determined not to go to the party and damning Zane's pending proposal.

"If I don't go to the Christmas party, I can return my new dress and shoes," Annie muttered as she entered her office.

"What? You aren't going? You're joking, right?"

Clarice was waiting for her, sitting at the workstation. Annie came to halt. Her office had been changed into a Christmas haven.

"I see you've been busy."

"I was. I didn't think I'd be able to do it. You never leave."

"It's lovely. Time always flies past me. I only finished decorating my home last night."

"Something special's been added this year."

She saw Clarice pointing at a mistletoe hanging from the top of the doorway. "Who put that there?"

"The office elves," Clarice whispered.

"Please have someone remove it. Such things aren't appropriate displayed over a VP's office."

Clarice shook her head no. "You'll have to get someone else to do it. I'm busy."

Annie stared at it. The festive atmosphere in the building had been in process since the employees arrived. All the limited edition Dollee dolls had been handed out. Christmas music played over the intercom, departments exchanged gifts, and there was a non-stop supply of food and cookies. However, Annie couldn't bring herself to join in the celebration.

"I'm not going tonight, period. I just can't."

"What? After all our planning. It's an extraordinary gift that Northern Polar Printing is different and is willing to give all its employees a grand celebration." Clarice grinned, then continued. "I look at this as a free little mini vacation. You've helped make up my mind. I'm upgrading my room, plus scheduling a massage. Lucy enjoyed one last year and the massage therapist was so sexy she experienced several orgasms."

"Clarice. Shhhh, someone might hear you, but it does sound delightfully sinful."

"I know," she purred and sighed. "You should make an appointment, too."

Annie watched her co-worker's face brighten. Weighing her own options, she remained silent and typed in the new numbers on the excel worksheet. Glancing at the totals she saw she'd keyed in several wrong amounts. Hitting delete, she retyped. Satisfied she'd entered them in correct, she pressed Save. Her concentration gone, Annie closed the laptop.

"Do you think I could pretend a sudden illness?"

Clarice didn't reply right away, but continued to flip through papers

75

for a moment. "I don't think the handsome Mister Santa with a very sexy day's growth of a beard, what's up with that, will let you go home. Or be a no show tonight."

"You know I don't tolerate office chatter," Annie said tersely. Her tone had no effect on Clarice who continued to babble.

"The two of you are meant for each other. Everyone in the company knows Mr. Ashcroft loves you. According to Starr who heard it from Fran—"

The ringing of Annie's phone halted Clarice's idle gossip and without hesitation, Annie answered it.

"Hello, Annie McGrath."

Clarice stood mouthing she'd return. Annie nodded and turned her attention to the phone call. The Christmas wish from a vendor was short. Replacing the receiver, she crossed her legs and arms. An image of the fortune cookie message, "love is real," wouldn't go away.

Was it?

She did love Zane. Everyone had a fight once in a while.

"Ready to go over the end of month spreadsheets?"

Annie blinked and pushed away thoughts of Zane. "Let's schedule time on Monday. Why don't you take the rest of the day off, Clarice?"

"It isn't even lunch time. The food hasn't arrived."

"Oh, right. See I'm just not myself."

"I'll bring you a plate. It should be here soon. Besides, I haven't printed the bonus checks so I can't leave. Can I start them?"

"Yes, I've settled the ledger and sent them to the queue."

Clarice went to the computer and pressed a few keys. "You never said what you're wearing tonight?"

"I um... it's a beaded... ah, I really don't want to go."

"You have to, Annie. You'll see. Everybody is meant to be happy. Why are you acting like the Scrooge? It isn't like you."

"I know... I know, I love this time of year. All the family spirit, the carolers, and the fruitcake. Even if I can only eat one piece," she paused and contemplated whether to reveal her reason. Folding her hands in front of her on the desk, she took a breath. "Zane is—he's to propose to me, tonight."

Clarice's eyes opened wide and put her hand to her cheeks.

"Propose to you? Tonight?"

"Yes, in front of everyone. I don't know what my answer will be. I never wanted to get married. It's never been in my plans."

"You love him. There's no way you can say no. You're going. Everything will be fine. Christmas time is full of miracles. I'm a believer," Clarice declared and walked over to her.

"Yeah, you're right. Maybe it's nerves. Can you believe that, me nervous? Disappointment is likely, unless I trust him—which I do, but—"

"Don't worry. This is so exciting. Why haven't you said anything? Does he know you know?"

"He told me months ago and again in today's card, Day Twelve."

"The man is so generous. No, he's very romantic. You'll have to act surprised for everyone. You still haven't said what you're wearing tonight? Something spectacular, I hope. You always do."

Embarrassed over Clarice's attention, Annie grinned hesitantly. "I bought a new gold beaded dress and new Jimmy Choo black pumps."

"You'll be the envy of all the women there tonight. My outfit isn't anything compared to yours. I found a blue velvet dress with silver beads around a scooped neckline."

The ringing of Clarice's phone interrupted before Annie could reply.

"Sorry, I'll be right back." Clarice hurried to her own desk.

Annie watched her retreating figure and studied the hanging mistletoe. This time it brought a smile to her face. She pushed the argument about Nick, from her mind. Her stomach did a flip at the prospect of being engaged.

"Eggnog?" Clarice held two mugs in her hands.

"Yes, time to enjoy the holiday fun," Annie agreed. It was time to mingle with the employees.

Chapter Nineteen

Opening the side drawer of his desk, Zane removed a little black velvet box. If it hadn't been for Clarice picking up the ring, he wouldn't have it right now. Mr. Yukon had offered to bring it to the office, but he hadn't wanted to take the chance of Annie seeing him. He'd called Clarice from the plane, and she stopped at the jewelry store before coming in this morning. She'd snuck into his office right after Annie had left.

Flipping the box lid, the three-carat pear shaped diamond engagement ring with baguette emeralds and the rubies flickered even without much light. He hoped she would like it. No, he wanted her to love it.

He knew Annie was angry again, but he hadn't had any choice. Nick was a problem. Chris had said there might be trouble, which was turning out to be true. Rudy's daily updates showed Nick was coming and going too freely.

He hadn't lied to Annie. The N & N Security, which was short for Naughty & Nice was more than a business entity of Mr. North's vast portfolio. They'd been running the background check. However, when he talked to Chris about the findings, he'd said he already knew Nick was his half-brother. He hadn't gone into detail, simply said he'd had it under control, but to have N & N Security step things up a notch.

Confused and not too busy to ask more, Zane let it go, which made it harder on him with Annie. It was something he couldn't yet share with her. They'd come full circle back to what had started their first major argument.

Trust.

The last two weeks hadn't happened the way he'd planned. There'd been the trouble with Nick, then Mr. North's disclosing unbelievable truths, and his two sudden trips to the most northern part of Minnesota.

Zane frowned. Annie's concern about Nick's strange behavior was warranted, but the stalking was another matter. The videos proved it. What bothered him was if Chris knew the reason, why hadn't he shared that piece of information? Was this how Annie had felt twelve days ago?

Understanding washed over him. It had been hard not to tell Annie when she already didn't trust him to share business decisions with her. Gaining her trust had been harder than he'd realized. Tonight she'll see his demonstration of love. With her trust and letting go of being in control, their relationship could last. He believed things happen for a reason and had a way of working out for them. He thrust Nick's problems out of his thoughts for the time being. N & N Security was on top of it.

Sounds from the employees' merriment drifted in. The song "The Twelve Days of Christmas" blared over the intercom, which had inspired his own rendition, The Twelve Cards Before His Proposal. His special plans had taken a new route since he'd begun preparation after last year's Christmas party.

"Any recycling?"

Zane looked up and lowered the box to his lap. Nick stood outside his office with his cart. "I don't have any recycling today. Have you been enjoying all the homemade treats?"

"No, sir."

"No? I thought for sure you'd be at the eggnog and spice cake."

"Not my cup of tea."

"If you should change your mind it's really good," Zane said. Dead silence followed.

Nick continued to stare at him. A crazy mixture of anxiety and tension built in Zane as he tried to keep things under the radar, not wanting Nick to know he was on to him.

"Can I help you with something?"

"I...no, sorry to have bothered you," Nick said, shrugging his shoulders and moving past the doorway.

79

The man was on borrowed time.

Zane moved the box and the diamond sparkled. Their relationship had been anything, but normal from day one. She'd literally shocked him their second night out of town on business, by asking if he'd be interested in having sex. He knew better than to get involved with a fellow employee, but she'd been so forward and attractive he couldn't say no. They'd gone full throttle with no regrets ever since.

"Excuse me, Mr. Ashcroft," Sammie his secretary said. "I have Fantasy Costumes on the phone. Would you like me to take a message?"

He glanced at his watch. Time was against him today. His bachelor hours were numbered.

He smiled at Sammie and straightened. "No, put it through."

Snapping the box closed, he put it in the drawer as the phone beeped.

"Hello, Mr. Ashcroft speaking."

"Hi, this is Fantasy Costumes. Your Santa suit is ready. We close at four today."

"Okay, I'll be over in less than an hour. Thank you," he replied and disconnected. In one fluid motion he rose and stepped into the hallway. "Sammie, I have to leave for an appointment. Has the Hyatt confirmed all my plans?"

"Yes." She smiled. "It should be an extraordinary evening."

"I appreciate your help. You don't have to wait for my return."

"The bonus checks haven't come from accounting."

"I'll get them myself from Ms. McGrath," Zane said.

"Thank you, I could use some extra time. My daughter is coming over to house sit Dash, my mini Yorkie."

"That's nice of her. Remind me later to give you a gift card for her."

"It isn't necessary," Sammie replied.

"I know it isn't, but she's being nice and that goes a long way in my book."

"Thank you, I will. She'll love the gift. I'll leave then in a couple of minutes. Thank you again."

"You're welcome, I'll see you later."

She smiled and nodded.

Nice? Book? Is it happening already? Mr. North and Mr. Moonracer said it wouldn't take effect until after Christmas Eve.

Uneasily he called Mr. North.

"Hello, Zane."

"Chris, I think it's starting early. I haven't asked Annie yet. I don't—can't do this without her."

"I should've warned you. You'll experience small changes. I feel mine slipping away."

"I've also somehow started growing a beard."

"I forget about that," Mr. North tittered. "It's been such a long time ago since I was chosen. We'll talk more when I arrive for the party."

"Okay, I'll hold it together. I have a lot of questions."

"I'll answer them the best I can, goodbye for now."

"Goodbye." He replaced the handset.

Zane headed to Annie's office. As he approached her door, mistletoe hanging overhead caught his attention. Zane leaned against the doorframe, arms crossed over his chest.

"Ms. McGrath, what time should your sleigh be waiting for you this evening?"

She was eating from a plate of desserts and set the cookie back before looking at him. No smile adorned her beautiful face, but she took his breath away.

"What time is good for you?"

He heard the forced pleasantry in her voice. She was a hard woman when she got mad, but he could almost guarantee she'd melt in his arms later.

"Let's plan on five-thirty. Be ready or be square." His humor didn't work, only the corners of her lips twitched.

"Okay, five-thirty it is."

Annie stood. Her navy blue suit added to her natural beauty. He motioned for her to come closer. She did and before she could guess why, he gathered her into his arms and without hesitation kissed her lips. Their earlier one had only been a mere touching of lips. This time he moved his over hers passionately, showing her how much he missed her. Immersed in the moment, Zane pressed his body against hers, their desire and rapture escalated.

"Ummmm, excuse me, do you really think that's a good idea?"

81

He opened his eyes and ended the kiss as Annie's body went rigid. She pushed at him, but he refused to let her leave his arms just because an employee decided to interrupt them.

"Good afternoon, Clarice. Yes, kissing the woman I love was a very good idea. You shouldn't have hung a mistletoe here, if people aren't expected to take advantage of it. I don't want to discriminate. Would you care for one, too?" Zane said and then whispered in Annie's ear. "I'll make good on that promise your lips are begging for."

"No," Clarice said. "I'm staying away from that doorway now." She giggled and backed out into the hallway.

Zane laughed, too, kissed Annie's lips once more, and let her move from his arms. "Leave the checks on my chair. Five-thirty, Princess."

Winking at the two stunned women, he walked away. She has to say yes tonight. He couldn't live without her.

Chapter Twenty

"Wow. I could feel the sizzle all the way over here. I bet he's a good kisser," Clarice said to Annie.

"Yes, he is and that's all I'll admit."

She'd realized the instant his lips touched hers, she'd forgiven him. How he did it, she didn't know, but he put her in a daze each time he gathered her close. It was the two of them in their private world of thundering arousal. She inhaled to calm her racing heart.

"I'm glad we printed the checks when we did. We can leave when we want. It'll give us extra time to prepare for tonight."

Clarice clapped her hands. "I was hoping you'd say that. From the looks of the empty desks all the departments thought the same thing."

"Did you find a new dress to wear?"

"I told you this morning, Annie. Don't you remember? It's a really sexy blue velvet dress. It has silver beads around the neckline. It looks like these things,"—Clarice pointed to her breasts—"are encased in diamonds."

"Oh, huh," Annie answered, but wasn't paying attention. She took a few more deep breaths and lightly touched her lips. He wasn't a good kisser. He was an exceptional one from the velvety warmth of his lips to their demanding caresses.

The trust she'd struggled with the last plus week made sense now. Like his card had said, "Without their past, they had no future." Every lasting relationship had to consist of mutual respect. As undesirable as marriage was to her, the prospect of having Zane all to herself, sent a warm glow through her and a sense of unbound joy.

83

"I'm ready. Are you?"

Annie blinked. She still stood in the doorway. "Yeah, give me two minutes. I was thinking of…"

Clarice laughed. "I would've, too. He's a handsome man. I know you don't like to gossip, but have you talked to him about Nick?"

Walking to her desk, Annie shut down her laptop, and slipped it into her briefcase. "I have. His concern isn't the same as mine. The old men verses women thing."

"When I find a man, he better be my knight in shining armor all the time."

"That would be nice. I guess I'm being paranoid. Too vivid an imagination," Annie murmured.

"My father is always tough on his students. He says, it'll make them into better men. I'll find a good one someday, too."

"I think Zane is a keeper. I fell in love and didn't really know how much I'd miss him until we had our argument. Maybe I'm having a mid-life crisis."

"Mid-life?" Clarice replied. "You're still young. Love is always around the corner. My mother's words of advice is that you just have to run into it to find it."

"I know what my answer is going to be, but what if I've ruined my chance of Zane proposing to me tonight?"

"Good Lord, after the kiss I just witnessed, Mr. Ashcroft has a good idea what your answer will be. He'll be on Santa's good list for sure after tonight."

"Santa? That's nonsense. You're talking like you believe Santa's real." Annie shook her head.

"I do and so should you." Clarice nodded and wrapped her red scarf around her neck.

They walked through empty hallways and past the conference rooms. The building had turned into a ghost town. When they stepped into the warehouse, it, too was almost empty.

"Clarice?"

Stopping, Annie moved backward as Rudy came from behind his station.

"Hi, Rudy," Clarice said shyly.

"Ummm… the company holiday party." Rudy paused. He cleared his throat a couple of times and inhaled. "Will you save a dance for me?"

Annie took another step to the side grinning from ear to ear.

Clarice gave Rudy one of her famous friendly smiles. "If the right song is played, I will."

"Awesome. I'm looking forward to claiming that dance."

"Okay, see ya later," Clarice said. "Come on, Annie. Time is a wasting."

"See you tonight, Rudy," Annie muttered and restrained her laughter at his very evident infatuation with Clarice. Rudy had been so frazzled. The poor guy's face had turned a little red spreading to his nose, and he kept his eyes averted from Clarice's exposed bust line.

The midafternoon sun wasn't warm and only intensified the cold. Chin lowered, Annie snuggled into the collar of her coat. Clarice walked to the only other car in the lot.

"Why don't you give Rudy a chance?"

"Who says I'm not."

"Oh, I guess I missed that, too."

They laughed for a moment and Annie pushed her key fob. Her BMW lights flashed.

"I shouldn't say this, but be kind to him. He's cute for a guy his age."

"Okay, okay," Clarice snickered. "I have to admit he is gorgeous in his uniform. I'll change the seating arrangements and have him sit next to me, but, no dancing. There, happy now?"

"We'll see if you keep your promise. As you said earlier, this is the time for everyone to be happy. You'll be giving him a very special Christmas present."

"Ho, ho, ho," Clarice chanted, as she opened her car door. "Catch you later."

Noticing Zane's car wasn't next to hers, Annie removed her cell phone from her purse and called him.

"How's my Annie girl?"

"Well, hello to you, too," she said and laughed. "I'm leaving for the day. Is there a problem? I didn't know you left."

"Everything's fine," Zane said. "Had to swing by the Hyatt to confirm the final arrangements for tonight."

"Do you need me to do something?"

"No, I checked the ballroom. It's a winter wonderland, Annie. It brought back memories of when I was a kid. Oh, and I reserved our room for the whole weekend."

"I beg your pardon." The line went silent and she checked to see if she'd lost the signal. "Zane?"

"I love you, Annie. I'll do anything to prove it to you. Don't forget, five-thirty."

"Okay, Casanova. I love you, too." Annie couldn't help but smile as the call ended. With the car door open, she remembered she'd forgotten Clarice's present in her desk drawer and to put the bonus checks on Zane's desk. She set her briefcase on the floor behind the driver's seat, clicked the key fob to lock the doors, and returned to the warehouse entrance.

"Ms. McGrath, can I help you?"

"No, Rudy. I forgot a few things."

"Okay, the log says everyone else has left. Would you like an escort? Only the afterhours lights are working."

"Thanks, but no worries. I'll be fine."

He nodded and held open the door.

An eerie quietness greeted her. She'd gotten used to it over the years after numerous late nights. Without the Muzak playing, the chatter of employees, or the hum of the computers, the area was a different world. She turned the corner and saw Nick go into her office. She frowned. Annie opened her mouth to call to him, but didn't.

When she reached her doorway, she observed Nick rummaging through her desk. Annie halted in her tracks and reversed her steps. She froze once she'd cleared her door.

What could he be looking for? Everyone knew the petty cash was in the safe in Zane's office.

Afraid to go any further, she reached inside her coat pocket for her phone, but couldn't find it. Had she left it in her car or purse? Panic seized her. The sound of a drawer slamming halted her movements. An instant later, Nick nearly ran into her. His look of surprise said it all.

Taking command of the moment she spoke first. "Oh my goodness.

Nick? You scared me."

"Ms. McGrath...you aren't.... Can I help you?"

His tone had no emotion. The hairs on her arms rose. He still blocked her path. The silence lengthened.

She shifted to pass him. "I... I left the recycle box under the table. I forgot to bring it to the warehouse. You know, I don't like to be a slacker."

It was a bold face lie. She never took it to the warehouse. She chewed her bottom lip hoping he wouldn't catch it.

"No ma'am, you're always good. I'll take care of it for you."

They stood staring at each other for an awkward moment.

Annie cleared her throat and continued into her office.

"Thanks. Sometimes I'm so forgetful."

To her horror, he followed her, but bent and took the box.

"Nite," he sneered and left.

Annie released the breath she'd been holding and heard him whistling. Her hands trembled as she searched a second time for her phone. She found it deep inside the lining of her coat. The pocket she'd put it in had a hole. Digging into the depth of the hole, she recovered her phone and called Zane. It rang and rang, then went to voicemail. Tapping 'End Call', she tucked her phone into her other pocket. She swallowed hard waiting for her nerves to quiet.

Nick had to be fired. No, ifs or buts about it. Zane was going to have to do it. It wasn't acceptable to have an employee go into her desk or anyone's for that matter.

She took everything in at once and didn't notice anything missing. Going to her desk, she took Clarice's gift and the undisturbed stack of checks from the top of her desk. Returning to the hallway, she didn't see Nick anywhere in the area. She went to Zane's office and set the checks on his chair.

Taking one last look around the entire area and not seeing Nick, she headed for the exit.

"Rudy, did you see Nick come this way?"

"No, I thought he'd left. Let me see..."

Annie waited by his station as he typed.

"Oh, he's still logged in. Says he's working until five. Did you want me to page him for you?"

"No," she smiled. "How late are you working?"

"Six o'clock. I might be a little late tonight, but I won't miss my first company function."

"I'm glad you're able to attend. I'll see you there." She hesitated a moment. "Clarice is looking forward to that dance."

"Oh she is? Thank you, ma'am."

She nodded and hurried from the building, taking several glances over her shoulder to make sure she wasn't being followed.

Chapter Twenty-One

Zane let up on the gas pedal as he drove into the empty parking lot at three-forty-five and chuckled. His first Christmas with the company he'd tried to cancel the lavish holiday party, but Mr. North refused despite warnings it could be detrimental to the bottom line. In retrospect, he understood how wrong he'd been. The Christmas event was something he realized couldn't be dropped. It was too beneficial to the emotional well-being of the employees. Every year Annie voted to host it onsite to save the company money. He wondered what she'd say this year.

He parked his Porsche and hurried into the warehouse entrance shivering.

"Mr. Ashcroft," Rudy greeted him. "Did you forget something?"

Stomping his feet to clear them of snow, Zane unbuttoned his coat. "No, Rudy. My afternoon appointment went longer than I'd expected."

"The night lights are on. I can reset the main ones for you."

"No, that won't be necessary. I'll be fine."

"I want to thank you for extending the invitation to the N & N Security Company," Rudy said.

"You're welcome. I consider you part of the company. I'll only be a couple of minutes."

Opening the door, Zane went into the main area. Instead of going to his office he went to the restroom. Hand poised on the door, he stopped. A movement from the corner of his eye caught his attention. Scanning the hall, he didn't see anyone and proceeded into the bathroom.

As he left a few minutes later, he searched the area again. Not seeing anything out of the norm, he continued along the hallway.

"Mr. Ashcroft."

Zane pivoted in surprise. "Nick? You're still here?"

"Why wouldn't I be? I want to talk to you. I waited for you to return."

Nick's angry and harsh tone startled Zane. "What can I do for you?"

"I want answers!"

Pushing aside his overcoat, Zane put his hands on his hips. "Answers? To what? What's the problem?"

"Why couldn't you have let the company go bankrupt? It would've been for the best."

Zane had a hard time believing Nick was Mr. North's half-brother. The two didn't look alike or have the same temperament. Knowing Nick wasn't happy about the coming change and that he might try to ruin Christmas for everyone in the world, gave Zane the insight to take things more calmly.

"No employee should wish for their employer to go bankrupt," Zane said evenly. "Are you in financial trouble? Come into my office so we can talk."

"No!"

Zane retreated a step. Nick's one word had more anger in it than a pissed WWF Wrestler ready to explode. Trying a different approach, he changed the subject and chose his words carefully.

"It's getting late. Aren't you going to the party? You can relax, enjoy—"

"Are you stupid? You ruined my life. This should all be mine."

"Yours? What should be yours?"

Nick raised his hand. Zane didn't react in time and was knocked into the wall as Nick's hand met his shoulder.

"I want what's rightfully mine." Nick shouted and shoved him again.

Recovering from the initial shock, Zane pushed off the wall, hands fisted, ready for another attack, but Nick walked past him shaking his head.

"Nick, stop. Nick. Let's talk. How can I help you?"

His words had no effect. Nick didn't turn. He simply waved his hand in a salute.

"Mr. Pole. Nick," Zane yelled.

Nick disappeared around the corner. Zane followed him only to stop when he heard the sound of a door slam. Rubbing his hand over shoulder, Zane continued to his office assessing what he should do. The only thing to do was to let Mr. North know Nick was out of control.

On his chair he found the bonus checks and hastily signed each one, then slipped the stack and the precious little black box into his briefcase. He checked his phone and saw somehow he'd missed a call from Annie. It was timed stamped forty-five minutes ago. Instead of calling her, he called Mr. North first to discuss Nick.

"Hello, Zane."

"Chris, sorry to bother you."

"It isn't a problem. We just took off. What can I do for you?"

"Your earlier assumption about Nick... Sir, he's overstepped my comfort level. I'm concerned for your safety and the employees."

"I was afraid this might happen. Be assured I'll be fine. I've seen this coming for awhile. N & N Security will be on high alert from this point forward. Transition is never easy, especially when you aren't the chosen one."

"Chosen one? I don't understand. If, you have a half-brother, why wouldn't he be the next in line?"

"It doesn't work like a royal bloodline. It chooses the person."

Zane exhaled and shook his head. It was all, too farfetched for him to believe, yet all things pointed to a realm of mystery.

"Okay, be safe, and I'll see you at the party."

"My flight plan is to arrive by seven. Try to have a remarkable night."

"Yes, sir, I have the ring."

"She'll make a wonderful wife."

"Thank you. See you at the hotel. Goodbye."

"Goodbye," Mr. North responded.

Ending the call, an unexpected loud noise shattered the silence. Slipping the strap of his briefcase over his shoulder, Zane left his office. The whole area was quiet again, and he saw no movement. Heading to the warehouse, he took one last look around.

"Is this goodnight?" Rudy got to his feet and moved to the front of the counter.

"I thought I heard someone. Have you see Mr. Pole?"

"Nick?"

"Yes," Zane replied.

"No, I haven't seen Nick since Ms. McGrath asked about him before she left. I hope my reports gave you what you needed."

"They did. Thank you. Can you look to see if he's scanned his employee ID yet?" he said smoothly, with no expression on his face, but inward he seethed.

"Of course. Give me a minute." Rudy sat and typed on the keyboard. "He's still punched in. That's normal for him, sir. According to the log, Nick should be punching out in an hour."

"Can you tell where he is?"

Rudy moved to a set of monitors and scanned the cameras in different parts of the building.

"If he is still here, Nick isn't in the range of any of the cameras. I can try to move them to see if I can locate him."

"No, but if he should show up, please text me."

"Of course, Mr. Ashcroft. I'll let the nightshift know, too," Rudy said.

"Great. Thanks for your help," Zane responded with authority. "See you later."

The cold wind hit him as he hurried to his car. Once inside the vehicle, he checked his cell phone for the time.

Four-ten.

He still had time to stop at the store, Love is Everything, for a little extra spice for later.

* * * *

Once at Annie's house, Zane pushed open the door and removed his key. "Hello? Annie? I'm here."

"Just a minute."

He banged his feet together and rolled his shoulders to rid himself of the light snow. A delightful evergreen scent greeted him. The foyer had been decked out with Christmas decorations since he'd been here last.

A plate of cookies sat on the coffee table in the living room for Santa. Poinsettias lined the staircase wall and a four-foot snowman stood in the middle. Tiny mittens, ice skates, and elves with red scarves adorned the tree.

Zane sighed. She was perfect for him.

In midstride he stopped and cupped the doorknob. He debated if he should get the ring and propose to her now. A rustling sound broke his indecision and he turned.

"Oh, my God."

The words escaped sounding like a plea. Annie glided down the stairs in a form fitting gold sequined dress that shimmered in the low light. Her confidence and elegance destroyed his self-composure.

Why had he waited so long to make her his wife?

"You can close your mouth."

"Sorry, you took my breath away. If we had more time, I'd march you right up those stairs and lock the door."

Annie laughed and continued down the steps. "I'm sorry I got mad earlier. I'll make it up to you later tonight...uh, this weekend. I like your new unshaven look. It's very sexy."

"Have mercy on me. I want you right now. Can't I have a sampling?" His low throaty voice surprised him as he moved to the staircase.

When she reached the last step, she took his face in her hands, and her lips moved over his. Their softness smothered and melted the last hold he had on his desire. His arms encircled and lifted her from the step. Locked in an embrace their lips parted for a moment.

"Oh, Annie, I've missed you..."

Slowing, he lowered her until her high heels touched the floor. He reclaimed her lips in a caressing kiss. His thin thread of restraint nearly gone, he reached down to the hem of her dress and skimmed over her thighs and hips. Sliding his hand between her legs to the heat of her desire, he thrust fingers into her.

"Annie? No underwear?"

Her moans stopped his movements and he broke away from her tempting lips. Annie's smile said it all. She covered his hand with hers and drew it away from her warmth and then lifted it to her lips and kissed each finger.

His eyelids lowered as his hunger climbed to the point of no return and with his free hand pressed her hips to his, grinding.

"Do you want me to put on my Nice panties or do you want me to leave on the Naughty ones?"

She released his hand and pushed him in a gentle fashion. Zane moistened his lips, debating the outcome for a yes and no reply.

"Naughty ones will be fine," he breathed heavily and adjusted his slacks. "Wow, if this was the appetizer, I'm not sure I can wait for the main course and dessert."

"It's past five-thirty or did our plans change and you want to stay here."

"You're right, we better leave now, but every time I look at you I'll want you, just knowing you aren't wearing anything under your amazing dress." He distanced himself from her, bent, and collected her suitcase.

"You're killing me. I'm telling Santa, you've been bad."

"Go right ahead. I bet he'd approve."

"I didn't know you knew him so well."

Setting the suitcase down he held her coat, and she slipped it on. His fingertips brushed her bare shoulders wishing for the thousandth time they had time to make love. He kissed her shoulder before covering it with her coat. Holding open the door, he couldn't resist and ran his hand over the slight bulge of her well-shaped butt as she stepped in front of him.

"Nice," he said.

"No, Naughty," she articulated slapping his hand away.

They walked into the snowy night laughing. Inside the car Christmas music blared from the radio. He turned the knob to lower it and headed to the interstate.

"I don't want to ruin our night, but I returned to the office after we ended our call earlier and Nick was rummaging through drawers of my desk."

He slammed on the brakes and almost hit the car in front of them. What could Nick have been looking for in Annie's office? What if he became violent toward her?

"Did you see him? Or—"

"I know what I saw. It... He frightened me. I didn't know if I should've run or not."

Anger swept over him, and he clenched his jaw. "I saw him when I returned to the office. I've informed Mr. North. He's going... We'll get this problem taken care of real soon. N & N Security are taking steps as we speak."

He chose his words, not wanting to get into much detail, yet. Mr. North hadn't given him permission to divulge the big secret.

"What do you think he wanted? I don't keep any cash in my desk, and he would know where the safe was. He was totally surprised to see me standing outside my office. His scowl made my skin crawl."

"I'll change the company policy so that if anyone comes in after hours they need to go through security," Zane replied and tried to stay calm.

"I don't plan to anymore. The only reason I did was because I forgot Clarice's Christmas present and to drop off the bonus checks."

"Let's not let him ruin our weekend. He won't be working for us anymore. Period."

"It sounds so harsh—"

"It's over. No more discussion about Nick," Zane said.

"Oh listen to this song." Annie turned up the volume as the classic, "Santa Claus is Coming to Town," played. The mood in the car took on a lighter tone. "When I was little I'd wait all year for it come on television."

"Really? I preferred Dr. Zeus's, *The Grinch Who Stole Christmas*."

"Yuk, he was so mean and that poor dog."

Zane laughed. "But, he changed. He became Santa."

"I never looked at it that way."

"I guess we still have a lot to learn about each other. I want to know everything about you." He chuckled at her discomfort.

"Stop it. That was when I was a kid. Christmas is more for them than for adults. Anyway, when you stopped by the Hyatt, did they have a table set-up for check-in?"

"Yes, plus my favorite chair is positioned for the guest of honor's arrival," Zane chuckled.

"The big red Santa Claus throne you used the past couple of years?"

95

"Yes, and I delivered the Santa suit earlier to our room."

As they neared the River Road exit, he reached over and slid his hand along the inside of her thigh and found her moist. His fingers did what he wanted to do but couldn't. Annie gasped, pushed her hand against his, and widened her legs. A red light worked in his favor. As he braked; he applied more pressure and drove deeper into the warmth. In a matter of seconds, she climaxed and was gasping when the light turned green.

Chapter Twenty-Two

Glowing from the raw act of passion, Annie savored the unspoken satisfaction he'd masterfully given her. Her yes answer was going to make this the weekend for their best ever sex.

"We're here. Should I park for a few minutes?"

Opening her eyes, she saw the hotel. Her body still warm from the sweet ecstasy.

"No, I'm fine," she said. Adjusting her dress and coat, she applied lipstick.

Zane maneuvered the car into the valet lane and waited.

"Welcome to the Hyatt Regency O'Hare Hotel." A young man held open the passenger's side door.

Annie shifted her legs to the side ready to exit, but Zane appeared and offered his hand, which she accepted.

"Will you be checking in?" the valet said.

Zane turned to him. "Yes. We'll be checking into the VIP Suite. Last name, Ashcroft."

"Yes, Mr. Ashcroft. We've been expecting you."

Annie stared at Zane. "We don't need a room that large."

The VIP Suite? What was he thinking? Last year the Regency Suite, was more than enough.

"You shouldn't have," she whispered.

"Only the very best for my Annie," he murmured.

Zane raised her hand to his lips and brushed a kiss on the top. She stood, staring into his brown eyes and blushed. Her pulse quickened at the electricity of his touch, reminding her she was pantiless and of the intimacy they'd just shared moments ago. His nearness was stifling in spite of the cold. Her coat became a hindrance, craving the feel of his hands on her. Maybe we do have time for a quickie.

"I want you, too." His soft-spoken voice close to her ear was a caress.

For the love of diamonds was she that transparent?

Wrapped up in his nearness, it wasn't until they arrived at the Front Desk counter that she saw the spectacular Christmas decorations.

A twenty-foot artificial Christmas tree took over the entrance, reaching to the third floor. A ginormous Gingerbread House was assembled in the restaurant area and a delightful smell of fresh baked cookies scented the air.

"Zane, maybe we do have—"

"Annie." Clarice called as she rushed up to them. "Annie, I'm so glad you're finally here."

"Hello, Clarice," she chuckled at her co-worker's excitement.

"Forget all the formality. There's no way you can envision it," Clarice declared and winked at Zane. "The sign says *Santa's Wish List*. Downstairs, the ballroom isn't a ballroom. It's Winter Wonderland, Santa's cottage, and the huge oversized red velvet chair from last year is ready for when Santa arrives,"

"As soon as we check in, I'll head downstairs," Annie said. "I have to help Zane with a couple things first."

"Okay, but hurry. It's, soooooo marvelous… No, spectacular. You have to see it." Clarice turned away and almost ran to the escalator, her blue dress a blur.

"She's so excited and you were impressed, too. I'm curious now."

"I hope you like it. Later, Santa can make your special wishes come true," Zane promised.

"No wonder Clarice is so taken by the decorations. She believes in Santa you know."

Zane's eyebrows rose. "And you don't?"

A hotel employee cleared her throat. "You're all checked in. If you need anything, Mr. Ashcroft, Holly Blitzen, your personal concierge, will be here in a half hour."

"Thank you. Can you page me when Mr. North arrives?"

"He has already."

"That's not possible," Zane protested.

"Just a moment," the employee replied and began typing. "I've doubled checked and he has. Would you like me to ring his suite?"

"No. Just let him know I'm here," Zane replied.

Annie watched the exchange, noticing how fidgety he appeared. Again, thoughts that he was keeping secrets from her came to the forefront, but thrust them aside, wanting their night to be memorable.

"Yes, sir. Can I help you with anything else?"

"No, thank you."

"Enjoy your stay Mr. Ashcroft and Ms. McGrath."

"Why don't you go ahead and see what Clarice needs," Zane said as he led her toward the escalators. "I can finish the other things on my own. I have to meet with Mr. North soon."

"Are you sure? We could make use of our room for a quickie."

She impishly dropped her hand from his waist to slide it over his butt and gave it a squeeze.

"Don't tempt me, Annie. I can only take so much," he whispered and kissed her. "Later, I promise."

"Okay, but I might not be so easy then."

He laughed. "Here's the keycard in case you need it. You have to hold the card up to a little box by the buttons in the elevators and then press floor twenty-four."

"I shouldn't have to go to the room. I'm dressed for our extravaganza. Come down as soon as you can." She leaned over, kissed his cheek, and then wiped the telltale lipstick.

"I love you."

Annie smiled and proceeded to a gigantic old fashion scroll of paper with script writing on it by the escalator. Before disappearing she glanced in Zane's direction and caught him staring at her and gripped the handrail as a flood of wantonness coursed through her. Later she'd get her fill of him.

The escalator ended and an array of oversized toys greeted her. Huge stuffed bears in Santa hats, dolls of various sizes, vintage and new style bikes along with large cookies lined the walkway into the ballroom.

In the past, the room had become "The Twelve Days of Christmas,"

Christmas trees, and Santas from around the world, and *The Nutcracker*, with all types of nutcrackers had decorated the room and tables.

A huge smile spread across her face at the sight of the North Pole recreation. Clarice was right once again. Tonight was destined to be magical.

* * * *

Zane exhaled. The sight of Annie walking away hammered at his heart. He'd turned down having an afternoon of delight. Good Lord, he must be in love.

A grin overtook his mouth. With his hands in his pockets, he returned to the registration counter. "Thank you for not spilling the beans."

"You're welcome, Mr. Ashcroft, Holly was very explicit in her notes. So to ensure Ms. McGrath doesn't have access to the room, I gave you bad keys. Here are good ones."

Zane's face came alive with delight. She set two keys cards on the counter. "You're good. Thanks again."

"It's my pleasure. I left your message with Mr. North. He asked me to tell you to come up to his suite, twenty-four-twenty-four."

"Great."

With long purposeful strides, he avoided several of the Northern Polar employees who called out greetings. Nodding to them, he reached the elevators. The glass doors slid open. Zane held his keycard to the pad, and pressed twenty-four. He unzipped his briefcase, insuring the black box was safely inside.

Chapter Twenty-Three

Annie found Clarice sitting at a table just past the Santa's Toy Wish List entrance, distributing nametags. Seeing the long line of employees, she joined her. At first things were a little chaotic with so many people arriving at once. When the rush diminished, she reveled in all the compliments. For the first time, she really understood how important the party was to all the employees and their spouses.

She sighed. "Wow, almost everyone is checked in."

"Oh my. Almost everyone," Clarice breathed wistfully, sounding more like a moan. "Where is a mistletoe when I need it?"

Expecting to see Zane, Annie faced the escalator. Instead it was, Rudy O'Deere, walking toward them, dressed in a dark brown suit with a red tie featuring an old-fashion Santa. Clarice stared at him, tongue-tied.

To cover-up her co-worker's surprised expression, Annie greeted him. "You made it in time. We haven't started yet, Rudy." She handed him his nametag.

"Thank you. Traffic wasn't too heavy."

Clarice still made no sound and simply stared at him.

"I like your suit," Annie said and nudged Clarice.

"It's new. I hope my tie is okay, I went for fun."

"I love it. Clarice, why don't you show Rudy around."

Annie kicked her beneath the table.

"Ouch—"

"I hear the appetizers on the table with the reindeer ice sculptures are extraordinary, but, save room for the main course."

"Are you sure, Annie? Shouldn't I stay?" Despite mumbled words,

101

Clarice rose, smoothing her dress which only accentuated her shapely body.

"Ma'am, I'd like that very much."

"Go on, I can manage the few late arrivals. Besides, I'm waiting for Zane and Mr. North," Annie said, shooing Clarice from behind the table.

Clarice's blue dress flowed around her like ripples of water. She hadn't lied about the sequins displaying her Double-D girls.

"Mr. O'Deere, shall we?"

"With pleasure. After you." He offered his arm.

Clarice's eyes widened at the show of gentlemanly etiquette. The chemistry between the two sizzled in the air. Annie had a feeling they'd be a couple soon. Arm in arm they walked into the ballroom like royalty.

Sighing at the sight of them and the new budding love, she wondered what had happened to Zane. With the party starting in thirty minutes, she paced back and forth. Checking her phone, she didn't have any missed calls or text messages and then saw the no-signal icon. Ten minutes passed, and then twenty. Noise from the ballroom drifted to her, and she couldn't help but take a peak.

Everyone was laughing, drinking eggnog and hot chocolate, and eating canapés. The dinner tables featured a miniature gingerbread house for each guest. White covers with large red ribbons covered all the chairs and a pine cone with a spray of evergreens decorated the backs. At the far end of the room, two ice sculptures, a gingerbread boy and a gingerbread girl, adorned the dessert table.

All the holiday traditions and celebration sparked a memorable moment of time that would be etched in her mind forever. Why tonight? How was the merriment different for her?

She couldn't pin point. Things appeared brighter, more lavish than in the past. The night was going to be perfect for Zane's proposal.

"The hotel surpassed last year's event. I've never seen anything like this before."

Annie turned to see one of the last employees approach her. "It is lovely, Fran. Everyone's raving about the cup of hot chocolate from Mrs. Santa Claus."

"Hot Chocolate? It's a favorite of mine. I'll try one for sure."

They moved back to the greeting table and she gave Fran her

102

nametag.

"I want you to know how much I look forward to this every year. Not many companies still care about their employees as much as Northern Polar Printing does."

"Mr. North will be here. If you get a chance, let him know, too."

"I'll do that."

Fran went into the ballroom, leaving Annie alone again. She glanced at the escalators, hoping Zane would be there, but no one else came. Anxious to join the festivities Annie left her post.

The first thing she did was go see Mrs. Claus who handed her a hot chocolate topped with marshmallows. Once there, she couldn't ignore the treats. Taking a plate, she added two strawberries cut to look like a Santa with whipped cream as the beard.

Waiters and waitresses mingled among the crowd asking everyone to take their seats. Her good mood verged toward dissipating. She went to her assigned table where Clarice and Rudy were already seated. They didn't even acknowledge her as she set her plate and drink down.

Glancing over at the entrance, she saw Zane. Her heart fluttered. He'd changed from his work suit into a black tuxedo.

"Excuse me," she mumbled and rushed to him, anxious as a teenager.

"Zane, you're late."

Standing eye to eye, she touched her lips to his in a brief kiss. His hand rested on her waist.

"Sorry we took so long. I—we—have to talk. I mean Mr. North—I—have to talk to you."

"Good evening, Ms. McGrath. No need for the same greeting."

Annie turned and felt her cheeks grow warm. She hadn't seen Mr. North behind Zane. The large man wore a red tuxedo. How she'd missed that she didn't know. Ready to move out of Zane's embrace, but he wouldn't let her. He gathered her closer against his side.

"Sorry, sir," she said.

"No need to apologize or be embarrassed. He's all yours for the weekend. Mr. Moonracer will be joining us shortly, too. I see everyone is enjoying themselves."

Three sets of eyes looked over the crowded ballroom. The company employees were indeed celebrating.

"They are," Annie agreed with pride. "I have you seated at table twenty-five, over to your right. You will be sitting with myself, Zane, Clarice Donner, and Rudy—Rudolf O'Deere, and I'll have another plate set for Mr. Moonracer. I'm excited to meet him."

"Nice. Next year, please no more mention of moving the Holiday Party off-site."

Annie lowered her head for a moment. "Yes, sir. I've come to understand the importance of our Christmas Party. The money Grinch has left."

"I'll mingle for a bit." Mr. North chortled, patted her arm, and winked at her before walking away.

In that instance she was reminded of the Santa's helper at the mall. Yet could it have been Mr. North? She dismissed the thought as Zane's hand slid lower over her hips. Her pulse quickened. He leaned in and she felt his breathe on her ear.

"Nicely said. Can I claim responsibility for softening your heart?"

The huskiness and his erotic southern drawl aroused flames, again reminding her of her naughty panties. "I'll never tell," Annie replied sweetly and kissed him.

"Before we join everyone, I need to talk to you."

"Zane, don't ruin our night. I love you."

"I love you, too, but, I have to discuss something very important with you. We might have more of a problem with Nick—"

"Shhhh…" She put her fingers to his lips. "No more talk of him, or business. Do we have time for a quickie?" She lowered her hand from his face to his white shirt. Its coolness contrasted to the burning she felt. "Maybe the bathroom…"

"You're being a bad girl again," he teased, lowering his hand from her waist to the contour of her backside in a caress. "Dinner has begun. We'll have to wait."

"I don't like being on Santa's Nice list," she pouted.

"You don't know how tempted I am." He laughed and hand in hand they walked to their table. Once seated, Mr. North joined them and as if on cue, a waiter brought Caesar salads.

"Clarice, I believe you've met Mr. North," Zane said. The two nodded. Then he continued. "Rudy, this is the owner of the company. Being your first Holiday party with us, what do you think?"

"Sir—Mr. North, it's...it's very nice. Thank you for inviting me."

"I, too, wish to welcome you, Rudy. Please call me Chris instead of Mr. North. It's, too formal."

Annie half listened to the conversation, noting it took on a light fun tone. Rudy and Chris formed an instant friendship talking sports and weather. Clarice, she noted, hadn't said a word and couldn't keep her eyes off Rudy. Every so often she touched his hand. He in turn, would smile at her.

Zane however, was another matter; at every chance his hand was beneath the table caressing her leg and the inside of her thigh. Each touch ignited a hunger and increasing her eagerness to be alone with him such as she'd never felt before. The casual attitude he portrayed to everyone, surprised her.

Wasn't he affected by desire, too?

Self-satisfaction pursed his mouth, but in her cocoon of desire she could only stare at him with unsatisfied longing.

Just before the main course of Cornish hens arrived, so did Mr. Moonracer. The Go To Meetings live stream video of him hadn't done him justice. In person he was a very handsome, burly man.

"I'm sorry I'm late," Mr. Moonracer said. "Last minute details during the busy season." His English accent and his demeanor of an aristocrat charmed Annie. She was surprised she hadn't noticed it the other day.

Annie rose and held out her hand. "Good evening, I'm Annie McGrath."

"Ms. McGrath, please sit. It's my pleasure to meet you. We have a lot to discuss, but not until Monday. I plan on staying the entire week to keep you busy." They shook hands and Annie sat.

Zane began the introductions. "I'd like to introduce you to Clarice Donner, who works with Annie and Rudy O'Deere, an employee, of N & N Security."

"Nice to meet you both."

Clarice and Rudy both mumbled a greeting to Mr. Moonracer as he took the vacant seat next to Mr. North. While they ate, they had a lively

105

discussion of which old toys should be brought back for children.

As the dessert platters of cookies were served, Zane rose to his feet. "Please excuse me. I believe I heard a noise on the roof. I'd better go check."

Everyone laughed. He kissed Annie's cheek before leaving and Rudy also excused himself.

She leaned into Clarice to whisper. "I'm frazzled right now."

"Don't be. When is he going to do it?"

"I don't know. What if he doesn't?" Annie folded and unfolded her hands.

"I'm betting he does when he calls your name to get the bonus check. This is so enchanting. I'm so tickled to be a part of this."

"You're no help, besides that won't happen cause I don't get one," Annie said and adjusted her dress. "I need another hot chocolate and I'm adding a shot of Amaretto. I'm so nervous."

"Nervous? You, Ms. McGrath?"

She covered her mouth with her hand. "Yes. I think Zane is going to propose to me."

"Hoo, hoo," Mr. North chortled. "I told you Santa had a plan for you."

"You sound as if he's real," Annie responded. Clarice snickered.

Annie glared at her and then turned back to Mr. North. "We're both, too old for that, but—"

"My, my Annie." Mr. North reached across the table and tapped her hand. "It's real if you believe."

"Is she a non-believer? That's can't be," Mr. Moonracer protested.

"She'll be one. Time says she will," Mr. North replied.

"Time? I don't mean to be rude, but you two are not making sense. I believe in the Christmas magic," she confessed.

"See, all things will come together," Mr. North said proudly.

Shaking her head, Annie smiled. "I see we're at a stalemate. Would either of you like a hot chocolate or coffee?"

"I would like a coffee with a shot of Baileys in mine." Mr. North smiled.

"No, thank you," Mr. Moonracer said. "I've just received a text message. Please excuse me."

"I'll join you Annie." Clarice rose.

As they zigzagged around tables making their way to Mrs. Claus and the hot drink station, Annie saw Rudy return to the ballroom. He waved at them and went toward their table.

Mrs. Claus held a black carafe, "What can I get for you young ladies?"

"Two hot chocolates with Amaretto and a coffee with Bailey's."

"Goodness, are we being naughty?"

"No," Annie and Clarice chimed in at the same time.

"I won't tell if you don't. I like a little something after Santa goes to bed."

They laughed at Mrs. Claus' confession. A male elf added the liquor to the cups and candy cane cookies to the saucer.

"Thank you."

"Merry Christmas," Mrs. Claus said and winked.

"Rudy seems to have swept you off your feet," Annie observed as they moved away.

"He has. I can't explain it, but tonight—I mean he's very sweet and such a gentleman." Clarice released an audible sigh. "You're right. I just might break my rule of no dancing."

Annie gave Clarice an approving glance. "See I knew—"

She stopped, her words lost, as she saw Santa coming from behind a curtain. Her heart began to pound so hard she thought she might faint.

This was it. Her life was going to change. She shuddered and swallowed hard.

"Annie, what's wrong?"

"It's Zane—Santa, he doesn't—"

"Everyone stay where you are and no one will get hurt."

A half-smile froze on Annie's face. Why was Zane holding a gun? No, the Santa held a gun. Her heart skipped a beat. There was no way that man was her Zane. If it wasn't him, where was Zane?

Everything happened in slow motion. Clarice screamed and dropped the cups of hot chocolate. More people cried out. Fear knotted Annie's insides. A shiver of panic surfaced, then a disturbing thought that Zane was hurt, or worse dead, shattered her resolve.

"BE QUIET," the Santa shouted and stepped into the middle of the room as co-workers scattered. "Mr. Norrrthhhh, where are you?"

Annie poked a frightened Clarice and whispered, "Let's move slowly to our table. We'll be safe there."

They took small steps, trying to avoid attention, as they moved across the crowded room. Clarice's fingers dug into her arm. Rudy nodded at her to keep coming in his direction.

"Oh where, oh where, are you?" the Santa called out pointing the gun at employees as he passed them.

Once she and Clarice were within a few feet of their table, Rudy moved in front of them providing a shield.

The armed Santa progressed slowly around the room and then halted at Mrs. Claus's station. "Have you seen him?"

Mrs. Claus shook her head.

The fake Santa laughed cruelly. "As if you'd tell. The real Mrs. Claus died years ago. I knew her."

He sauntered to the Gingerbread House. "Anyone home? Mr. North, you can't hide from me. I want what should be mine."

From nowhere Zane emerged from behind curtains minus his tuxedo coat and rubbing his head. She almost yelled out to him as their eyes met across the room. He shook his head and ducked out of sight. Her chest hurt from holding her breath as she waited for him to reappear.

"I see you, Mr. North. You've been a very bad boy. Ho, ho, ho, ho," the imposter Santa chanted. He strolled toward the four of them, gun pointed. Employees hastily shifted aside, some ducking under the tables as a path formed.

"Everyone be quiet!"

This time it worked, the room grew quiet with a tenseness on the verge of erupting.

"What do you want? You're frightening people," Mr. North exclaimed, rising to his feet. "Why don't you..."

Clarice clung to her arm. Annie kept glancing at Zane, who was darting around tables and people. Rudy shifted closer to Mr. North, but he waved Rudy off.

Santa leveled the gun at Mr. North as he approached. "Ho, ho, ho. What do you think I want?" he said in a creepy gremlin tone.

Hand in hand Annie and Clarice backed away until chairs halted their progress. Annie lost sight of Zane.

"This isn't the time or place to air our problems," Mr. North responded in an attempt to reason with the imposter Santa.

Annie flinched; impressed Mr. North didn't look scared or worried.

"Come now, dear Brother. Yes, it is. It's time for everyone to know what you really are," the false Santa snapped.

Annie inhaled sharply. Santa turned the gun on her.

"What's wrong, Ms. McGrath? I thought for sure you'd put two and two together," the imposter crooned and yanked down the long white beard.

"Nick?"

The name echoed in the room followed by gasps.

"The red head is smart after all—"

"Nick, what are you doing? It's been explained to you. If you needed something, you should've come to me," Mr. North said.

Now Annie gripped Clarice's hand harder, releasing the breath she'd been holding as Nick aimed the gun at Mr. North again. Beyond them, Zane progressed meticulously against the far wall. In what seemed a lifetime to her, he arrived a few feet from their table. Zane glanced at Rudy, who nodded and revealed a gun tucked into the waist of his pants. Without having to say anything, Zane's eyes told her to be ready.

"You're living in a fantasy world, *Brother*. Now you show—"

Then it happened. Zane grabbed the Santa's hand holding the gun. They struggled. An ear piercing gunshot echoed through the ballroom. Clarice screamed. Annie released her hand as Rudy pushed past them and pushed Mr. North to the floor. Zane held a fighting Nick on the ground, the gun thrust away from everyone in the room.

"Get off me. I have every right to talk to my brother," Nick gasped out the words, thrashing his head upward.

"Terrorizing people and shooting a gun, isn't talking," Zane snapped.

"It's your fault, too. You should've let the company go bust and I would've gotten my revenge on my so-called half-brother. The world needs to know—"

"That's enough. You've threatened the employees of Northern Polar Printing too many times." Zane shoved Nick's face down and held his arms behind his back.

Mr. North scrambled to his feet with Rudy's help and walked to stand over Nick. "It wasn't meant to be. You knew it would never be yours."

"It could have. You—"

"Stop, Nick," Mr. North demanded. "I'm sorry, Zane. I should've dealt with this better. The transition is never easy on the family."

Mr. North bent down and pulled off Nick's red velvet hat while Zane continued to hold him. Mr. North smoothed back Nick's hair and touched his cheek gently.

"Soon it won't matter, Nick, my brother. Time isn't our friend anymore."

Annie strained to hear what was being said. Her forehead creased. Time? Mr. North was losing it. What was 'IT'?

Getting to his feet, Mr. North clapped his hands. A scent of sugar cookies filled the air. Annie watched, as everyone in the room appeared to be in a daze. Zane glanced up at Annie. She shook her head, confused by the whole scene. The cookie aroma vanished, but she stared at Mr. North and then Zane in awe.

The new and old.

Beginnings and endings in the same room.

All the things she knew to be real weren't. The things she thought to be simply a childhood fantasy indulgence were real.

Mr. North was Santa and Zane was to be the next one. Then it was gone. She shook her head to clear her mind.

"What's going on, Mr. Ashcroft? Why am I on the ground?"

Nick's sobs broke the special link she'd been seeing. Other employees close by seemed to come out of their daze.

"Everyone move aside. We'll take it from here."

Two police officers and several security guards confiscated the gun and led a perplexed Nick from the ballroom in cuffs.

Annie searched for Clarice realizing she wasn't next to her anymore and gasped in terror. Her co-worker-friend was leaning against the wall holding her arm. Blood oozed through her fingers. Grabbing cloth napkins from the table, Annie paid no attention to the commotion around her and held them to Clarice's wound.

"I need help here. Clarice has been shot."

"I've been shot? I thought something hit me."

A pale, Clarice, moaned and crumpled to the floor.

"Hang in there." Rudy knelt next to Clarice gathering her close. "You still owe me a dance. You aren't getting out of it that easy."

Clarice blinked and gazed at Rudy. "Are you my knight in shining armor?" She half-smiled and fainted in his arms.

"We need help over here," Zane yelled.

Paramedics came rushing over and lifted Clarice onto a gurney. Rudy held her hand. She awoke disoriented.

"You fainted," Annie explained. "They have to take you to the hospital."

"I don't want to go alone. Where did my knight go? Will you come, please," she begged.

Clarice's ashen face was defined by fear. Annie looked over at Zane being inspected by additional paramedics.

She glanced back at her friend. "I will, give me a second."

"Annie, go. I've been given an all clear. Don't worry," Zane promised and hugged her. "Rudy and I can manage everything here. They're saying the bullet just grazed Clarice."

Tears threatened, but she kept them at bay. "I was so afraid something happened to you when I realized the Santa wasn't you. Then the gun went off. I couldn't see—and Mr. North and you—"

"Annie," he hushed her.

A lone tear escaped as more threatened. He framed her face with his hands. "I'm fine. Go on, take care of Clarice. We have a lot to talk about when you get back. I told you Santa is real."

She sniffled and kissed him. "I love you."

The paramedics began to push the gurney. She followed them leaving behind the chaos.

111

Chapter Twenty-Four

Returning to the Hyatt around one a.m., Annie noted most of the police cars were gone. She'd had hours to comprehend all the information she'd been given somehow. Mr. North was Santa, but his time of being the beloved figure was over. The miracle had chosen to take over Zane for this role while she'd been handpicked to be his Mrs. Claus. The newness of the whole situation remained unbelievable.

Inside, several employees rushed over to her. She assured everyone Clarice was fine and Rudy was with her at the hospital. Annie excused herself and headed to the escalator to the ballroom, but yellow crime scene taped blocked it. An officer nodded to her. Turning around, she went to the elevator, and held the key card to the pad.

Nothing happened.

She repeated and still nothing.

"Damn," she muttered and marched to the registration desk. Her prior enjoyment of her Jimmy Choo shoes gone, replaced by pain, aching feet, and wanting them off never to see them again.

"Ms. McGrath, may I help you?"

Annie recognized the woman from earlier. "Yes, my key card didn't work in the elevator."

"I'm sorry. I'll get you a new one. I heard no one was seriously injured."

"Yes, it's very fortunate. The employee that was hurt should be released in the morning. Please deliver a huge basket of fruit and a couple bottles of wine to Ms. Clarice Donner's room and bill it to Northern Polar Printing."

112

"Of course, but the Hyatt will do so as our gift to her."

"Thank you so much." Annie sighed.

She shifted from one foot to the other. Fatigue and exhaustion mounted a private war inside her. The magical moment that should have happened, hadn't.

"Sorry for the wait, the computer is slow. I also have a message for you."

The woman handed her an envelope. Annie broke the seal and read it.

Annie,
I'll be in our room waiting for you.
Love, Zane

A part of her came alive. The comfort of his words lifted her spirits. In her earlier haste to leave, she'd forgotten her evening handbag with her phone in it on the table and hadn't been able to talk to Zane.

"Here you go, Ms. McGrath. Again, so sorry for any inconvenience."

"Thank you." She strolled to the elevators in a daze, as her last energy drained. This time when she placed her key card to the pad it blinked and she was able to press button twenty-four. The doors closed. The chaos in the grand foyer vanished and, for the first time in hours, she allowed some of the tension to fade away.

The doors opened and she went to room twenty-four twenty-five. Sliding the key into the slot the green light flashed and she pushed the door.

"Oh my lord."

Annie stepped backward to check the room number. She tilted her head in confusion. Christmas spectacular greeted her. Garland, ornaments, a life-size Frosty the Snowman, and a Christmas tree with tinsel and lights everywhere completed the brilliance of the display.

"Hello?"

"Ho, ho, ho."

"Zane?" She stepped into the room. "Oh my."

The love of her life sat in the oversized red velvet chair from the ballroom. Gone was his tuxedo except the black bow tie, his bare upper torso magnificent. Shocking red satin boxers completed his so-called outfit. One leg swung over the arm and the other on the floor.

Oh good Lord.

She blinked a couple of time. "Don't you want to sit on Santa's lap?"

"Have you lost your mind? Maybe I should take you to the hospital, too?"

Zane laughed, placed both feet on the floor in front of him, and beckoned her with his finger. In slow deliberate steps she went to him and kicked off her now hateful shoes.

She giggled when he patted his knee. Her eyes glued to the gap in the red boxers, revealing his thick and ready man business. She hiked up her dress in an unladylike manner and straddled him.

Face to face, his arms tightened around her and they kissed. His tongue demanding and exploring the recesses of her mouth. She battled his tongue in a sexual way, savoring the fight. A hunger sang through her; gone was the weariness. She felt his erection pushing against the inside of her thighs.

"I don't remember Santa ever being this sexy," she said and touched his muscular forearms and then his chest.

"This is the adult version."

His hand caressing her thigh moving higher until his fingers stroked her. She moaned, closing her eyes. A tremor of desire heated her thighs and groin. His other hand tugged at the zipper of her dress. It loosened and he lowered his head, kissing the exposed swell of her breasts.

Being naughty had its advantages.

"I want you, now," she heavily moaned.

His assault ceased. The whirl of growing passion raged through her. She opened her eyes and peered into his. Then his fingers nestled between her thighs, pushed into her, sending a delightful surge of pleasure coursing through her.

"I want you, too, but first…" He withdrew his fingers and lifted her weightlessly into his arms as he stood. "We have to make this perfect."

If this wasn't perfect she didn't know what would make it. Gone were her worries of Clarice, Nick, Mr. North, and the whole ambiguity of Santa. He carried her to the bedroom. She wrapped her arms around his neck, enjoying the feel of his naked chest. The king-sized bed was turned down and in the middle of the pillows was a black box.

"Zane?"

He stopped. She felt every contour of his lean body as her feet touched the floor, arms still around his neck. They separated inches, her arms falling to her side. He tugged the zipper the rest of the way and her golden dress floated to her feet.

"You really are naughty tonight."

"I wanted to make sure I made it on Santa's Nice List."

"Oh, you have Annie," he said hoarsely and once more lifted her. Setting her on the bed, his hands caressing her. He lay next to her and added. "This isn't how I planned to propose to you."

He nestled his fingers around her full and soft breast. His tongue lapped at one rosy peak. Her nipple firmed and he repeated his pleasurable assault on her other breast. She sighed and parted her legs.

"Annie," Zane breathed and brushed a strand of her hair from her face. "I have loved you from the first moment we met. Sometimes I was frightened by all the emotions you made me feel, but I now know it was because I didn't want to lose you." He reached across her and opened the black box. Taking the ring, he took her hand. "Will you be my wife? My Mrs. Claus?"

The cold metal marked its way down her finger. The last hours, weeks vanished. Tears she'd held broke free. "I love you, too. Yesssss—yes."

To seal their vow, their lips met in a gentle kiss. A spark, like an electric current coursed through them. They stared at each other. Their world changed in that instant.

The magic took hold. She saw everything. All of history's past Christmases flooded her mind. Mr. North delivering presents to homes. Mr. North and Mrs. North working to make wishes come true. Years and years of the two of them being Santa and Mrs. Claus. Then Mrs. North died and sand in an hourglass clock poured into the bottom glob.

She felt Mr. North's heart wrenching sadness. Before a tear could fall, an overwhelming joyous feeling took her breath away. A book Mr. North was flipping through lit up. Pages flew to one side and then stopped. Her name seemed to come off the sheet of paper.

"Zane?"

"Annie?"

"What just happened?"

Zane kissed her. "I tried to tell you earlier. Chris said time would explain itself."

"But, the Santa—It can't be true. You're the big guy?"

"I guess—yes. Annie can you feel the magic?" He smiled.

"I can. It's unbelievable. I'm Mrs. Claus! Who would've even known?"

"You're going to be a wonderful Mrs. Claus. With your business expertise we'll be able to leave our mark on history by change. Mr. North will be our teacher for a short time before the magic leaves him. We'll have to find someone to take over Northern Polar Printing," Zane said.

"I'm still processing all the information."

Zane took her hands and placed them on his chest. "I love you."

"I love you, too."

They kissed and the world spun. His hand moved downward lightly outlining her nipple with his fingers. She tugged on his satin boxers.

He helped and pulled them off, tossing the boxers on the floor. She snuggled against him as their legs intertwined. Passion pounded through her and she yielded to the burning desire as he nested his arousal against her warm and moist mound. In one sensuous thrust, his hardness filled her.

Turbulent quivers vibrated through her soft core sending swirls of rapture within her. When their flames came to an uncontrollable burn, he kissed her hard and took his own release.

They lay drained in the glow of rapture, each in their own private heaven of wonder. He rolled to his side, kissing the tip of her nose.

"Let's get married on Christmas."

"Okay, Santa. Then you'll always be my present."

Annie beamed, knowing she had a true life Santa that would make all her wishes come true. Zane didn't give her much time to rejoice as he kissed her neck sending additional rounds of exotic bursts throughout her body as the smell of cookies filled the air.

The End

About the Author
Sonja Gunter

Born and raised in the cold and beautiful Minnesota, she escaped to Illinois for seventeen years to raise two boys, and now calls Florida home. She and her husband Andy, who's always her hero, have a new family to worry about; Cookie, an Assui-Po dog, Oreo, a black and white cat who thinks he is a dog, and Chip, a ragdoll cat, that their sons compare to Eeyore.

She loves to travel, read, and bowl. You can catch her writing her next novel at the lanes.

Sonja encourages you to check out her web site, www.sonjagunter.com, for more info and don't be surprised if she lets her Norwegian heritage come through in her stories. You betcha!

http://sonjagunter.com/

www.ingramcontent.com/pod-product-compliance
Lightning Source LLC
Chambersburg PA
CBHW031840170626
46807CB00004B/1544